BOOKS BY ERIC AMBLER

TO CATCH A SPY (editor)   1965

A KIND OF ANGER   1964

THE LIGHT OF DAY   1963

PASSAGE OF ARMS   1960

STATE OF SIEGE   1956

THE SCHIRMER INHERITANCE   1953

JUDGMENT ON DELTCHEV   1951

JOURNEY INTO FEAR   1940

A COFFIN FOR DIMITRIOS   1939

CAUSE FOR ALARM   1939

EPITAPH FOR A SPY   1938

BACKGROUND TO DANGER   1937

To Catch a Spy

An Anthology of Favourite Spy Stories

Edited and Introduced by

Eric Ambler

ATHENEUM NEW YORK

1965

All rights reserved
Introduction and notes copyright © 1964 by Eric Ambler
Library of Congress catalog card number 65-15044
Printed by Halliday Lithograph Corporation, West Hanover, Massachusetts
Bound by H. Wolff, New York
First American Edition

CONTENTS

ERIC AMBLER

Eric Ambler was born in London in 1909. Following his graduation from London University, he served an apprenticeship in engineering, toured England as a vaudeville comedian, wrote songs and, for several years, advertising copy. In the period from 1937 to 1940 Mr Ambler produced four of his most successful novels: *Background to Danger*, *Cause for Alarm*, *A Coffin for Dimitrios* and *Journey into Fear*. He joined the British Army in 1940 and was discharged a lieutenant colonel in 1946, having been in charge of all military-training, morale and education films for the Army. After the war Mr Ambler left off writing novels to write and produce a number of motion pictures for the J. Arthur Rank Organisation. For his screenplay of Nicholas Monsarrat's *The Cruel Sea* he was nominated for an Academy Award. In 1951, *Judgment on Deltchev*, his first novel in eleven years, was published. This was followed by *The Schirmer Inheritance* (1953), *State of Siege* (1956), *Passage of Arms* (1960), *The Light of Day* (1963) and *A Kind of Anger* (1964). Mr Ambler lives in Bel Air, California.

Introduction

by
ERIC AMBLER

◆

The sudden emergence, in the nineteenth century, of the detective story has been satisfactorily accounted for by a distinguished American critic, Mr Howard Haycraft. Having reminded us that crime detection, in the modern sense of the term, was a nineteenth-century innovation, he goes on: 'Clearly, there could be no detective *stories* until there were detectives.'

The belated arrival of the spy story is less easy to understand.

Prostitution may, as we are told, be the oldest profession, but that of the spy cannot be much younger. There seems to have been no period in recorded history when secret agents have not played a part, and sometimes an important part, in political and military affairs. And yet, it is impossible to find any spy story of note written before the twentieth century.*

The usual explanation is that, until the Dreyfus case (1894–99) brought such matters so sensationally to the public's attention, nobody had been much interested in spies or spying, and so would not have been interested in stories about them.

This seems to me too simple, and, in its suggestion that the public cannot be interested in stories about unfamiliar subjects, plainly silly. Mr Haycraft, obviously feeling the need for a

---

* James Fenimore Cooper's *The Spy* (1821) is mainly concerned with conflicting loyalties during the American War of Independence. It is noteworthy only in that it is unreadable.

7

sociological explanation of the phenomenon, suggests that it was 'a logical literary by-product of the cumulative politico-military stresses' of the time. However, he leaves it at that; and we are left to guess what he means by the word 'logical', and wonder why the considerable politico-military stresses of the Napoleonic era did not produce a similar result.

Is there any satisfactory explanation? I believe that there may be; but I think that it lies in the eighteenth century rather than the nineteenth. The significance of the Dreyfus case in this context rests, in my opinion, not so much on its having created a new public appetite or whetted an unfamiliar curiosity, as on the fact that it re-opened a discussion which had been firmly closed for nearly a hundred years.

Until the Hague Convention of 1899, the 'rules' of war had generally been determined by 'custom'; and, of course, that did not mean very much. It might be the custom of one army to torture and kill its prisoners, and of another to enslave them. The rules varied with the players. However, during the eighteenth century, throughout which Western Europe was in an almost constant state of war, a sort of common-law convention was established. For sanction there was the unwritten military code of honour that had evolved from the medieval practices of chivalry.

The code of honour transcended nationality; it was a discipline of a quasi-religious character; and if it was often absurd (duels, of course, were affairs of honour) it was more often useful and humane. Such things as truces for the succour of wounded, exchanges of prisoners, flags of truce and *paroles d'honneur* could only be negotiated between belligerents who could rely upon one another's good faith. The code was very real. An officer was a man of honour and his word of honour had to be believed. If he lied or cheated, then he was dis-

8

honoured and damned. As Clausewitz, surely no romantic, put it, 'Honour can only be lost once.'

On the subject of spies, however, the code was evasive and ambivalent. If you caught an enemy spy, your conscience was clear; you were entitled to hang the wretch on the nearest tree. But what about the spies you employed? Was your association with them compatible with the spirit of the code? The military men of honour could only hedge.

Napoleon said that one spy in the right place was worth twenty thousand extra men in the field. He was speaking of one of his own spies, Schulmeister, a man of great courage, skill and loyalty. But, when the time came to reward Schulmeister for his services, it was the same Napoleon, a stickler for the proprieties in some matters, who refused him the Legion of Honour, remarking contemptuously that money was the only suitable reward for a spy. The same Napoleon had not hesitated to ennoble Savary, one of the murderers of the Duke of Enghien, nor to reward the odious Fouché with the Duchy of Otranto; but a spy was different; no spy could be a man of honour.

And no military man of honour would degrade himself by becoming a spy; at least, not willingly. The case of Major André demonstrates how far unwillingness could go.

It was during the American War of Independence. The fortress of West Point was then 'the key to America', in Washington's own phrase, and its capture by the British could have resulted in the Americans losing the war. When, therefore, the American commander of West Point, General Benedict Arnold, let it be known that he was prepared to betray the fortress to the British for £20,000, the British commander, Sir Henry Clinton, jumped at the chance. All he had to do was to send a reliable agent who would negotiate the deal with the traitor, discuss the planning and timing of the *coup* and then report back to headquarters. For this critically important mission, General Clinton chose his adjutant-general, Major André.

The meeting place chosen by Arnold was a house on the Hudson river not far from the fortress. Secret agent André went there by boat. Incredibly, he also went wearing his British Army uniform.

Almost immediately, things went wrong. André reached the meeting place safely, but American gunners along the river had spotted the boat, which flew British colours. Soon, they brought it under fire and forced it to retreat down-stream. There was only one way now for André to get back to British headquarters with the fruits of Arnold's treachery: he would have to ride overland through an area extensively patrolled by trigger-happy American irregulars.

Yet, even in that predicament, he was still reluctant to give up his uniform, put on civilian clothes, and so become a 'spy'. He had to be persuaded, presumably by Arnold. Finally, he agreed; but his agreement was half-hearted, for, while he accepted a civilian coat, he clung, pathetically, to his military boots and breeches.

On his way back, he was stopped by an American patrol. The boots aroused suspicion and he was searched. The compromising papers that he was carrying completed his downfall.

He was court-martialled, convicted of being a spy, and sentenced to death by hanging. General Clinton wrote to General Washington claiming, on the somewhat peculiar grounds that his agent had gone to meet the traitor Arnold under a flag of truce, that André ought to be treated as a prisoner of war. However, Washington, a steady employer of spies himself but also a military man of honour, refused to intercede.

The execution aroused some indignation on both sides of the Atlantic.* André had not, it was argued, been in fact a spy, and had done nothing dishonourable. When 'disguised' he had merely been attempting to avoid capture. After all, if it were a legitimate *ruse de guerre* (and the British said it was) for a ship to wear false colours in order to confuse an enemy or avoid capture, why shouldn't an army officer carrying dispatches employ the same stratagem?

But André himself offered no such defence. Before his death, he wrote, resignedly, to General Clinton: 'The events of coming within an Enemy's posts and of changing my dress which led to my present Situation were contrary to my own Inclination as they were to your orders.'

He might, with reason, have bemoaned his carelessness, or even his bad luck. He did neither. As a man of honour he could only admit to inexcusable misconduct. It is interesting to note that he had no compunction about dealing with a traitor who wanted money for his treachery; perhaps he felt that the uniform made that all right. Paradoxically, if he were tried to-day under the Hague Convention rules, Article 29 would acquit him of espionage, as he was not 'seeking information'; but he could be convicted of negotiating 'war treason'.

A good spy, as we have already seen, can be brave, skilful and loyal; but those attributes alone are not enough for success. He must also have considerable strength of character. Spying is lonely and often depressing work. The spy's friendships can only be warily professional. His appetites and weaknesses, even the small ones, must be rigidly self-controlled.

---

* George III considered André a martyr, and honoured his memory by granting a pension to his mother and a baronetcy to his brother.

He must be capable of living for long periods under exceptional nervous strain without cracking. Above all, he must be a man of absolute integrity where his employers' interests are concerned. He is, indeed, a very special type of civil servant.

But, admirable though he may be in terms of character and probity, the fact remains that, in his professional capacity, the spy is *ipso facto* a liar and a thief. He may be worse. It may be his business to suborn and corrupt, calculatedly to play upon the weaknesses of other men in order to make them traitors. He may have to use blackmail and extortion to get results. The fact that his motives are not those of a common criminal is beside the point. The motives of the public hangman are not those of a common murderer, but that makes it no more agreeable to shake hands with the fellow.

At least, that was how the old military men saw it. But theirs was a curious sort of high-mindedness: the thing they most objected to about the spy was that he concealed his identity. Their views on the subject of concealment were most eccentric. The word 'camouflage' had not then been taken into the military vocabulary, but the idea that it expresses was already known and detested. Again and again during the American wars regular troops had been roughly handled by frontiersmen, clad inconspicuously in buckskin, who, caddishly refusing to stand out in the open where they could be seen and killed, hid behind trees and sniped at the highly visible red-coats. Yet proposals for adopting a less conspicuous uniform (and different tactics, too) were always passionately opposed. Concealment was cowardice. The only concession to good sense made eventually by the British was the decision to form light infantry regiments for 'skirmishing'. They wore green coats with black buttons that did not glitter. The colonel of one unit converted to the light infantry role was so incensed by the change that he petitioned the King for permission to incorporate a red flash in the new uniform; he wanted all to know that his men were not trying cravenly to hide themselves from the enemy. The King's advisers saw his point immediately and the permission was granted. However, most British regiments retained their bright, glittering uniforms, as did the armies of the other European powers. It was not until 1884 that the British Army adopted khaki for service in the field. In some other countries the opposition to concealment died even harder. In 1914 the French infantryman was still wearing the blue coat and scarlet trousers that his grandfather had worn in 1870. They simplified the German machine-gunners' task considerably. The less visible blue-grey was not adopted until the following year, a million and a half casualties later.

When men greatly desire an end, but are ashamed of and despise the means to it, they have to seek an accommodation. There is an unspoken meeting of the minds—and an unspoken division of them, too. 'We know it has to be done, but we will not talk about it. We will give the orders if we must—though it is better if those who are to do the work will write their own orders—but we cannot participate. And we do not want to know how the results are obtained. Our hands must be clean.'

The outcome is usually a conspiracy of silence protected by a myth; and so it was in this case. Moreover, the protection was perennially reinforced by the security measures natural to any kind of spying activity. The silence was nearly absolute.

The myth was a simple one, and prevailed throughout the nineteenth century in most European countries. It held that spying was something that other countries did in time of war, and that, even if in self-defence one sometimes had to do a little spying oneself, no officer, no gentleman, was ever involved. Spies were always sneaking foreigners.*

Remarkably, most people believed it. Novelists and short story writers certainly did. It is even possible that the Prussian officers, disguised as tourists, who tramped the roads of eastern France gathering the information needed for the war plan of 1870, believed it, too; for by that time the myth had received embellishments. The terrorist activities of militant anarchist organizations and of secret societies such as the *Carbonari* had somehow (probably because they were also secret) become confused with espionage; so the sneaking foreign spy, with the false whiskers and his ear to a keyhole, now held a smoking bomb behind his back as well. It is hardly surprising that writers ignored the creature. The day of the anti-hero had not yet dawned; and there were difficulties about using him as a villain. If you acknowledged his existence at all, your hero would have to be some sort of secret service or counter-espionage agent, and, therefore, not much better than a spy himself.

To-day, when the man of honour is little more than a cultural curiosity, and cold war spy trials have become commonplace, it is hard to realize the sense of shock produced by the revelations in the Dreyfus case. After all, what did they amount to? Two civilized nations, France and Germany, nominally at peace with one another, were in reality waging a relentless secret war of espionage; the participants on both sides included high-ranking officers of the regular army; for political and

---

* In America, the War of Independence had produced a legend of the patriot spy (epitomized by Nathan Hale, who could 'only regret that I have but one life to lose for my country', before the British hanged him) but it was a legend that did not travel. When, towards the close of the 19th century the United States became engaged in foreign wars, they seem to have found it convenient to adopt the European myth.

personal reasons, but in the name of honour, quite a number of the French officers were prepared to lie, cheat and falsify evidence.

In France, as we know, the political and social consequences of the scandal were profound. The British reaction to it, however, was surprising. This was before the days of the *Entente Cordiale* and, as the Fashoda incident demonstrated, we were not on the best of terms with the French. It might have been supposed that the British would happily shrug off the whole affair as just one more proof of French decadence. Instead, the response was one of embarrassed indignation mixed with apprehension. Did we have some sort of *Deuxième Bureau*, too? No, no, of course not! Scotland Yard must deal with foreign spies and all that sort of thing. But Anglo-German naval rivalry was already in the air. If German officer spies could be at work in France, could they not also be at work in the British Isles? But the Kaiser was the Queen's grandson! The whole idea was unthinkable. All the same . . .

The German Fleet Law announcing the construction of a battle fleet was promulgated in 1900. Three years later the first spy novel was published. It was called *The Riddle of the Sands* and was written by an Irishman, Erskine Childers. The hero, Davies, is an intensely patriotic Englishman who likes 'mucking about in small boats'. Having combined a yachting holiday with some amateur spying he discovers that the Germans are planning the invasion of England by means of a fleet of troop-carrying barges based on the Frisian Islands. His companion, who tells the story in the first person, is a supercilious junior member of the Foreign Office. The villain is a renegade Englishman.

The Riddle of the Sands is still fascinating, not only because it is a good spy story, but also because it is one of the finest books about small sailing-craft ever written. At the time it had a serious propaganda purpose, which Childers explained in a postscript to the book. It was a sincere plea for naval preparedness to counter the growing German sea-power, and for the formation of an effective volunteer naval reserve. His English hero, Davies, was an idealistic patriot; and so was the Irishman, Childers. Having fought in the Royal Navy during the 1914–18 war, he went to Ireland and organized the very efficient I.R.A. intelligence network in Dublin. Later, after the Irish Free State authorities had outlawed the I.R.A., he was caught and condemned to death. He shook hands with the firing squad before he was executed.

Joseph Conrad's *The Secret Agent* (1907) was the first attempt by a major novelist to deal realistically with the secret war, with the sub-world of conspiracy, sabotage, double-dealing and betrayal, the existence of which had for so long been denied. The central characters are Mr Verloc, an *agent provocateur* employed by a foreign government to spy upon a group of exiled anarchists living in London, and his English wife, Winnie.

The Secret Agent is one of Conrad's acknowledged masterpieces, and it is difficult to discuss other spy stories of that period in the same breath. However, the names of William Le Queux and E. Phillips Oppenheim should be mentioned, if only because it was their enormous output that turned the spy story into a popular entertainment. Other writers imitated them. The early cloak-and-dagger stereotypes—the black-velveted seductress, the British secret-service numbskull hero, the omnipotent spymaster—were evolved at this time. *Donovan of Whitehall*, *The Invasion*, *The Czar's Spy*, *The Secret* and *The Mystery of the Green Ray* are the only Le Queux spy story titles that I can recall now, but there were dozens more. E.

Phillips Oppenheim was a much better writer. 'The Prince of Storytellers', as his publishers called him, he was a clever craftsman who manipulated a personal set of stereotypes with ingenuity and, sometimes, humour; and his improbable world of diplomatic salons, cosmopolitan hotels, and suave, stiff-, stuffed-shirted intrigue still has an engaging quality about it.* His best known spy story, *The Great Impersonation*, did not appear until 1920, and although it was a great success at the time, its manner was already becoming outmoded. The first of John Buchan's Hannay stories, *The Thirty-Nine Steps*, had appeared in 1915, and been followed a year later by *Greenmantle*. *Mr Standfast* had appeared in 1919.

Although, on the whole, Buchan's spy stories achieved a higher level of reality than those of Oppenheim, and were certainly better written, they had peculiar defects. His spy-heroes were mostly hunting-shooting-fishing men who went about their work with a solemn, manly innocence which could lapse into stupidity. They were also emotionally unstable.

Consider the scene in *Greenmantle* when Hannay, having at last convinced the brutal German intelligence officer, Stumm, that he is a pro-German South African, begins 'to see the queer other side of my host, that evil side which gossip had spoken of as not unknown in the German army.' When Stumm starts bullying him, Hannay suddenly loses his temper. In a sort of hysterical panic-rage, he beats Stumm into insensi-

* If this sounds patronizing, I would like to record my unqualified enjoyment, as a young man, of some of Oppenheim's novels which were not spy stories; notably, *The Amazing Quest of Mr Ernest Bliss*, *The Inevitable Millionaires*, and *The Double Life of Mr Alfred Burton*. It may be heresy to suggest it, but I don't think that Oppenheim really liked writing about spies. I think that his heart was with Prince Terniloff, his Ambassador in *The Great Impersonation*, who was made to say: 'You know my one weakness, a weakness which in my younger days very nearly drove me out of diplomacy. I detest espionage in every shape and form, even where it is necessary.'

bility and runs. By doing this he has not only rendered useless his carefully built-up cover story and made himself a fugitive in Germany, but also thrown away the chance to penetrate the German intelligence service for which he has been working so hard. Of course, Buchan alibis his man and makes it all turn out for the best; but one wonders what Mr Maugham's R, or Mr Fleming's M would have said about such neurotic and irresponsible behaviour.

In the early twenties, the spy story was mostly in the hands of Oppenheim, Buchan and Buchan's imitators. Some of Sapper's Bulldog Drummond books had counter-espionage themes; but they were very much in the blood-and-thunder department, with heroines always being tied to chairs by the villains, and the rescuing heroes shooting out light bulbs before they crashed in through the leaded-glass windows of the country house. Sapper did, however, introduce one dis- agreeable novelty to the British public. In *The Black Gang* (1922) Bulldog Drummond and some of his ex-officer friends get together to form a private strong-arm squad, dressed in black shirts and masked. The villains opposing them are left- wing politicians, militant trade unionists, and, of course, foreign Bolshies. Our hero's squad's way is to kidnap them at night, one by one, take them to some lonely spot and flog them within an inch of their lives. This makes the villains change their ways or leave the country. Scotland Yard shakes its head reproachfully over such goings-on, but secretly approves.

In 1928, Somerset Maugham's *Ashenden, or The British Agent* was published.

Some time ago, a *Times Literary Supplement* review of a reprint of *Ashenden* discussed the development of the spy story in general terms. It ended with these words: '. . . the detective story has its Simenon, the gangster novel its W. R. Burnett, the "serious" psychological crime novel and even the "serious" Western have their being; but the really realistic spy novel, as prefigured by *Ashenden* and Mr Ambler, does not as yet exist.'

This statement still bothers me, and for a number of reasons. The smiling inverted commas about the word 'serious' (is the writer applying a scale of values which he does not really believe to be valid?) are always vexing, of course; but the rest of it, unless the reviewer is quibbling that *Ashenden* is not a novel, but only connected short stories, I simply do not understand.

If *Ashenden* is not 'really realistic' and does no more than suggest that realism is attainable, then we are in semantic difficulties of some complexity. *Ashenden* was based, as Mr Maugham has told us, on his own experiences as a British agent in Switzerland and Russia during the 1914–18 war. It is thus the first fictional work on the subject by a writer of stature with first-hand knowledge of what he is writing about. As the same reviewer points out earlier in his article, 'Never before or since has it been so categorically demonstrated that counter-intelligence work consists often of morally indefensible jobs not to be undertaken by the squeamish or the conscience-stricken.'* Not really realistic?

And we are asked to accept some peculiar equations. Can it really be true that W. R. Burnett's *High Sierra* is more realistic or serious on the subject of gangsters than *Ashenden* is on the subject of spies? Does the detective story really have its Simenon? Or are detective stories and stories about detectives different things?

As for the flattering allusion to my own work, the reviewer points out elsewhere in the article that my early books were

---

* And he might have added intelligence work, too. *Ashenden* is concerned with both.

'strongly influenced by the *Ashenden* ethos'. They were, indeed. The break-through was entirely Mr Maugham's. If the reviewer was only expressing his regret that there has been no body of work in the field of the same quality written since *Ashenden*, then I am with him. I hope that that is really what he meant to convey. There is, after all, a lot of Simenon, and a satisfactory quantity of W. R. Burnett, but only one *Ashenden*.

There is, however, *The Three Couriers* by Compton Mackenzie. Published in 1929, it is clearly based upon Sir Compton's wartime experiences as Director, Aegean Intelligence Service, in 1917. I did not come across it until the forties; and could not understand why it had received so little attention. One explanation may be that it was at first overshadowed by the publication of his *Gallipoli Memories* in the same year, and then, when the subsequent *Greek Memories* had to be withdrawn because of a prosecution under the Official Secrets Act, allowed to go out of print.*

The Three Couriers consists of three overlapping stories linked by characters common to all three and by a developing political situation. It is more light-hearted than *Ashenden*. All highly organized military intelligence operations have an innate tendency to generate absurdity and farce. In *The Three Couriers*, the incidents and episodes that result from this characteristic are recorded with relish rather than irony. Sir Compton seems to have enjoyed intelligence work more than Mr Maugham.

Although spy stories have always been widely read in America, comparatively few of them have been by American writers. I don't know why this should be so. True, Helen MacInnes, whose *Above Suspicion* and *Assignment in Brittany* will be warmly remembered, is an American citizen; but she

* *Greek Memories* was reissued in 1940.

was born and educated in Scotland. The only American innovator in the field has been John P. Marquand, whose *Mr Moto* stories, most of which were published in the thirties, broke new ground with a Japanese central character and a fresh background, that of the Sino-Japanese wars. Mr Moto was a clever, ruthless and often highly convincing secret agent. After Pearl Harbor, not unnaturally, he dropped out of sight. Following a brief post-war re-appearance, in *Stopover: Tokyo*, he was permanently retired.

If it is possible to call Conrad's *The Secret Agent* a spy story (and I seem in effect to have done so) then I suppose that Graham Greene's *A Gun for Sale* (1936), *The Confidential Agent* (1939) and *The Ministry of Fear* (1943) should properly be placed in the same category. But now I am faced with the difficulty I have been trying to avoid. The development of the spy story does not present a single avenue of inquiry which can be simply traced and described. As Mr Anthony Boucher of the *New York Times* has pointed out, there is the spy story, and there is the story which happens to have a spy as protagonist. But *Ashenden* is a mingling of both. And what about the detective story which uses espionage as a motive for murder?

Of course, I should have started by defining the term 'spy story', if only for the purpose of this anthology. I did attempt to do so. I wrote: 'A spy story is a story in which the central character is a secret intelligence agent of one sort or another.' It is loose, but not too bad, I think. However, some critics say that I am a writer of spy stories, and the above definition would insist that I had never written a spy story in my life. While I could bear the disgrace, I think that it may be wiser perhaps to let the critics have it their way. Besides, if I had stuck to that definition, I should have been unable to include in this book Graham Greene's *I Spy*.

However, apart from that story, and one other, the stories here *are* about secret agents who are also central characters.

There are surprisingly few good *short* spy stories. If I could have my unfettered way, a spy story anthology would include *The Riddle of the Sands*, *The Thirty-Nine Steps*, all of *Ashenden*, all of *The Three Couriers*, plus Graham Greene's *The Ministry of Fear*, plus Ian Fleming's *From Russia With Love*, plus . . . but it is getting to be a rather heavy book.

Better not wait for it. Please begin now with the *hors d'œuvres*.

They are served in chronological order.

The Loathly Opposite

FROM 'THE RUNAGATES CLUB'

JOHN BUCHAN

◆

John Buchan was the son of a Scottish clergyman. When he died, in 1940, he was Baron Tweedsmuir and Governor-General of Canada. During his lifetime he had been, as well as a novelist and historian, a barrister, an army officer, a diplomatist, and a Member of Parliament. It was with professional men of that kind that he liked to people his novels, particularly the later ones.

In 'The Runagates Club', a book of short stories, he assembled a cast of such characters, drawn from the novels, and gave them a story apiece to relate. There they all are—Richard Hannay, Leithen, Sandy Arbuthnot, and the rest—reflectively sipping their port as they ruminate the treasured past.

The old device of telling a story as if the writer were merely an amanuensis setting down what he has heard from the lips of a friend was a favourite with John Buchan. He used it skilfully, too. The easy, circumstantial manner can obscure many improbabilities; and, even when it fails, you don't somehow blame Buchan; you blame the friend.

In this case, he is a senior army officer named Oliver Pugh, whom nobody would dream of blaming.

◆

How loathly opposite I stood
To his unnatural purpose.
King Lear

23

Burminster had been to a Guildhall dinner the night before, which had been attended by many—to him—unfamiliar celebrities. He had seen for the first time in the flesh people whom he had long known by reputation, and he declared that in every case the picture he had formed of them had been cruelly shattered. An eminent poet, he said, had looked like a starting-price bookmaker, and a financier of world-wide fame had been exactly like the music-master at his preparatory school. Wherefore Burminster made the profound deduction that things were never what they seemed.

'That's only because you have a feeble imagination,' said Sandy Arbuthnot. 'If you had really understood Timson's poetry you would have realized that it went with close-cropped red hair and a fat body, and you should have known that Macintyre [this was the financier] had the music-and-metaphysics type of mind. That's why he puzzles the City so. If you understand a man's work well enough you can guess pretty accurately what he'll look like. I don't mean the colour of his eyes and his hair, but the general atmosphere of him.'

It was Sandy's agreeable habit to fling an occasional paradox at the table with the view of starting an argument. This time he stirred up Pugh, who had come to the War Office from the Indian Staff Corps. Pugh had been a great figure in Secret Service work in the East, but he did not look the part, for he had the air of a polo-playing cavalry subaltern. The skin was stretched as tight over his cheek-bones as over the knuckles of a clenched fist, and was so dark that it had the appearance of beaten bronze. He had black hair, rather beady black eyes, and the hooky nose which in the Celt often goes with that colouring. He was himself a very good refutation of Sandy's theory.

'I don't agree,' Pugh said. 'At least not as a general principle. One piece of humanity whose work I studied with the micro-

24

scope for two aching years upset all my notions when I came
to meet it.'

Then he told us this story.

'When I was brought to England in November '17 and given
a "hush" department on three floors of an eighteenth-century
house in a back street, I had a good deal to learn about my
business. That I learned it in reasonable time was due to the
extraordinarily fine staff that I found provided for me. Not one
of them was a regular soldier. They were all educated men—
they had to be in that job—but they came out of every sort of
environment. One of the best was a Shetland laird, another
was an Admiralty Court K C, and I had besides a metallurgical
chemist, a golf champion, a leader-writer, a popular dramatist,
several actuaries, and an East End curate. None of them
thought of anything but his job, and at the end of the War,
when some ass proposed to make them OBE's, there was a very
fair imitation of a riot. A more loyal crowd never existed, and
they accepted me as their chief as unquestioningly as if I had
been with them since 1914.

'To the War in the ordinary sense they scarcely gave a
thought. You found the same thing in a lot of other behind-
the-lines departments, and I daresay it was a good thing—it
kept their nerves quiet and their minds concentrated. After
all our business was only to decode and decypher German
messages; we had nothing to do with the use which was made
of them. It was a curious little nest, and when the Armistice
came my people were flabbergasted—they hadn't realized that
their job was bound up with the War.

'The one who most interested me was my second-in-com-
mand, Philip Channell. He was a man of forty-three, about
five-foot-four in height, weighing, I fancy, under nine stone,

and almost as blind as an owl. He was good enough at papers with his double glasses, but he could hardly recognize you three yards off. He had been a professor at some Midland college—mathematics or physics, I think—and as soon as the War began he had tried to enlist. Of course they wouldn't have him—he was about E5 in any physical classification, besides being well over age—but he would take no refusal, and presently he worried his way into the Government service. Fortunately he found a job which he could do superlatively well, for I do not believe there was a man alive with more natural genius for cryptography.

'I don't know if any of you have ever given your mind to that heart-breaking subject. Anyhow you know that secret writing falls under two heads—codes and cyphers, and that codes are combinations of words and cyphers of numerals. I remember how one used to be told that no code or cypher which was practically useful was really undiscoverable, and in a sense that is true, especially of codes. A system of communication which is in constant use must obviously not be too intricate, and a working code, if you get long enough for the job, can generally be read. That is why a code is periodically changed by the users. There are rules in worrying out the permutations and combinations of letters in most codes, for human ingenuity seems to run in certain channels, and a man who has been a long time at the business gets surprisingly clever at it. You begin by finding out a little bit, and then empirically building up the rules of de-coding, till in a week or two you get the whole thing. Then, when you are happily engaged in reading enemy messages, the code is changed suddenly, and you have to start again from the beginning . . . You can make a code, of course, that it is simply impossible to read except by accident—the key to which is a page of some book, for example—but fortunately that kind is not of much general use.

'Well, we got on pretty well with the codes, and read the intercepted enemy messages, cables and wireless, with considerable ease and precision. It was mostly diplomatic stuff, and not very important. The more valuable stuff was in cypher, and that was another pair of shoes. With a code you can build up the interpretation by degrees, but with a cypher you either know it or you don't—there are no half-way houses. A cypher, since it deals with numbers, is a horrible field for mathematical ingenuity. Once you have written out the letters of a message in numerals there are many means by which you can lock it and double-lock it. The two main devices, as you know, are transposition and substitution, and there is no limit to the ways one or other or both can be used. There is nothing to prevent a cypher having a double meaning, produced by two different methods, and, as a practical question, you have to decide which meaning is intended. By way of an extra complication, too, the message, when de-cyphered, may turn out to be itself in a difficult code. I can tell you our job wasn't exactly a rest cure.'

Burminster, looking puzzled, inquired as to the locking of cyphers.

'It would take too long to explain. Roughly, you write out a message horizontally in numerals; then you pour it into vertical columns, the number and order of which are determined by a key-word; then you write out the contents of the columns horizontally, following the lines across. To unlock it you have to have the key-word, so as to put it back into the vertical columns, and then into the original horizontal form.'

Burminster cried out like one in pain. 'It can't be done. Don't tell me that any human brain could solve such an acrostic.'

27

'It was frequently done,' said Pugh.

'By you?'

'Lord bless you, not by me. I can't do a simple cross-word puzzle. By my people.'

'Give me the trenches,' said Burminster in a hollow voice. 'Give me the trenches any day. Do you seriously mean to tell me that you could sit down before a muddle of numbers and travel back the way they had been muddled to an original that made sense?'

'I couldn't, but Channell could—in most cases. You see, we didn't begin entirely in the dark. We already knew the kind of intricacies that the enemy favoured, and the way we worked was by trying a variety of clues till we lit on the right one.'

'Well, I'm blessed! Go on about your man Channell.'

'This isn't Channell's story,' said Pugh. 'He only comes into it accidentally . . . There was one cypher which always defeated us, a cypher used between the German General Staff and their forces in the East. It was a locked cypher, and Channell had given more time to it than to any dozen of the others, for it put him on his mettle. But he confessed himself absolutely beaten. He wouldn't admit that it was insoluble, but he declared that he would need a bit of real luck to solve it. I asked him what kind of luck, and he said a mistake and a repetition. That, he said, might give him a chance of establishing equations.

'We called this particular cypher "P.Y.", and we hated it poisonously. We felt like pygmies battering at the base of a high stone tower. Dislike of the thing soon became dislike of the man who had conceived it. Channell and I used to—I won't say amuse, for it was too dashed serious—but torment ourselves by trying to picture the fellow who owned the brain that was responsible for P.Y. We had a pretty complete *dossier*

28

of the German Intelligence Staff, but of course we couldn't know who was responsible for this particular cypher. We knew no more than his code name, Reinmar, with which he signed the simpler messages to the East, and Channell, who was a romantic little chap for all his science, had got it into his head that it was a woman. He used to describe her to me as if he had seen her—a she-devil, young, beautiful, with a much-painted white face, and eyes like a cobra's. I fancy he read a rather low class of novel in his off-time.

'My picture was different. At first I thought of the histrionic type of scientist, the "ruthless brain" type, with a high fore-head and a jaw puckered like a chimpanzee. But that didn't seem to work, and I settled on a picture of a first-class *General-staboffizier*, as handsome as Falkenhayn, trained to the last decimal, absolutely passionless, with a mind that worked with the relentless precision of a fine machine. We all of us at the time suffered from the bogy of this kind of German, and, when things were going badly, as in March '18, I couldn't sleep for hating him. The infernal fellow was so water-tight and armour-plated, a Goliath who scorned the pebbles from our feeble slings.

'Well, to make a long story short, there came a moment in September '18 when P.Y. was about the most important thing in the world. It mattered enormously what Germany was doing in Syria, and we knew that it was all in P.Y. Every morning a pile of the intercepted German wireless messages lay on Channell's table, which were as meaningless to him as a child's scrawl. I was prodded by my chiefs and in turn I prodded Channell. We had a week to find the key to the cypher, after which things must go on without us, and if we failed to make anything of it in eighteen months of quiet work, it didn't seem likely that we would succeed in seven feverish days. Channell nearly went off his head with overwork and anxiety. I used to visit his dingy little room and find him fairly grizzled and shrunken with fatigue.

'This isn't a story about him, though there is a good story which I may tell you another time. As a matter of fact we won on the post. P.Y. made a mistake. One morning we got a long message dated *en clair*, then a very short message, and then a third message almost the same as the first. The second must mean "Your message of to-day's date unintelligible, please repeat", the regular formula. This gave us a translation of a bit of the cypher. Even that would not have brought it out, and for twelve hours Channell was on the verge of lunacy, till it occurred to him that Reinmar might have signed the long message with his name, as we used to do sometimes in cases of extreme urgency. He was right, and, within three hours of the last moment Operations could give us, we had the whole thing pat. As I have said, that is a story worth telling, but it is not this one.

'We both finished the War too tired to think of much except that the darned thing was over. But Reinmar had been so long our unseen but constantly pictured opponent that we kept up a certain interest in him. We would like to have seen how he took the licking, for he must have known that we had licked him. Mostly when you lick a man at a game you rather like him, but I didn't like Reinmar. In fact I made him a sort of compost of everything I had ever disliked in a German. Channell stuck to his she-devil theory, but I was pretty certain that he was a youngish man with an intellectual arrogance which his country's débâcle would in no way lessen. He would never acknowledge defeat. It was highly improbable that I should ever find out who he was, but I felt that if I did, and met him face to face, my dislike would be abundantly justified.

'As you know, for a year or two after the Armistice I was a pretty sick man. Most of us were. We hadn't the fillip of getting back to civilized comforts, like the men in the trenches. We had always been comfortable enough in body, but our minds were fagged out, and there is no easy cure for that. My digestion went nobly to pieces, and I endured a miserable space of lying in bed and living on milk and olive-oil. After that I went back to work, but the darned thing always returned, and every leech had a different regimen to advise. I tried them all—dry meals, a snack every two hours, lemon juice, sour milk, starvation, knocking off tobacco—but nothing got me more than half-way out of the trough. I was a burden to myself and a nuisance to others, dragging my wing through life, with a constant pain in my tummy.

'More than one doctor advised an operation, but I was chary about that, for I had seen several of my friends operated on for the same mischief and left as sick as before. Then a man told me about a German fellow called Christoph, who was said to be very good at handling my trouble. The best hand at diagnosis in the world, my informant said—no fads—treated every case on its merits—a really original mind. Dr Christoph had a modest kurhaus at a place called Rosensee in the Sächsische Schweiz. By this time I was getting pretty desperate, so I packed a bag and set off for Rosensee.

'It was a quiet little town at the mouth of a narrow valley, tucked in under wooded hills, a clean fresh place with open channels of running water in the streets. There was a big church with an onion spire, a Catholic seminary, and a small tanning industry. The kurhaus was half-way up a hill, and I felt better as soon as I saw my bedroom, with its bare scrubbed floors and its wide verandah looking up into a forest glade. I felt still better when I saw Dr Christoph. He was a small man

31

with a grizzled beard, a high forehead, and a limp, rather like
what I imagine the Apostle Paul must have been. He looked
wise, as wise as an old owl. His English was atrocious, but even
when he found that I talked German fairly well he didn't
expand in speech. He would deliver no opinion of any kind
until he had had me at least a week under observation; but
somehow I felt comforted, for I concluded that a first-class
brain had got to work on me.

'The other patients were mostly Germans with a sprinkling
of Spaniards, but to my delight I found Channell. He also
had been having a thin time since we parted. Nerves were
his trouble—general nervous debility and perpetual insomnia,
and his college had given him six months' leave of absence to
try to get well. The poor chap was as lean as a sparrow, and
he had the large dull eyes and the dry lips of the sleepless. He
had arrived a week before me, and like me was under observation. But his vetting was different from mine, for he was a
mental case, and Dr Christoph used to devote hours to trying
to unriddle his nervous tangles. 'He is a good man for a
German,' said Channell, 'but he is on the wrong tack. There's
nothing wrong with my mind. I wish he'd stick to violet rays
and massage instead of asking me silly questions about my
great-grandmother.'

'Channell and I used to go for invalidish walks in the woods,
and we naturally talked about the years we had worked together. He was living mainly in the past, for the War had been
the great thing in his life, and his professorial duties seemed
trivial by comparison. As we tramped among the withered
bracken and heather his mind was always harking back to the
dingy little room where he had smoked cheap cigarettes and
worked fourteen hours out of the twenty-four. In particular he
was as eagerly curious about our old antagonist, Reinmar, as

he had been in 1918. He was more positive than ever that she was a woman, and I believe that one of the reasons that had induced him to try a cure in Germany was a vague hope that he might get on her track. I had almost forgotten about the thing, and I was amused by Channell in the part of the untiring sleuth-hound.

' "You won't find her in the Kurhaus," I said. "Perhaps she is in some old schloss in the neighbourhood, waiting for you like the Sleeping Beauty."

' "I'm serious," he said plaintively. "It is purely a matter of intellectual curiosity, but I confess I would give a great deal to see her face to face. After I leave here, I thought of going to Berlin to make some inquiries. But I'm handicapped, for I know nobody and I have no credentials. Why don't you, who have a large acquaintance and far more authority, take the thing up?"

'I told him that my interest in the matter had flagged and that I wasn't keen on digging into the past, but I promised to give him a line to our Military Attaché if he thought of going to Berlin. I rather discouraged him from letting his mind dwell too much on events in the War. I said that he ought to try to bolt the door on all that had contributed to his present break-down.

' "That is not Dr Christoph's opinion," he said emphatic-ally. "He encourages me to talk about it. You see, with me it is a purely intellectual interest. I have no emotion in the matter. I feel quite friendly towards Reinmar, whoever she may be. It is, if you like, a piece of romance. I haven't had so many romantic events in my life that I want to forget this."

' "Have you told Dr Christoph about Reinmar?" I asked.

' "Yes," he said, "and he was mildly interested. You know the way he looks at you with his solemn grey eyes. I doubt if

33

he quite understood what I meant, for a little provincial doctor, even though he is a genius in his own line, is not likely to know much about the ways of the Great General Staff . . . I had to tell him, for I have to tell him all my dreams, and lately I have taken to dreaming about Reinmar.'

' "What's she like?" I asked.

' "Oh, a most remarkable figure. Very beautiful, but uncanny. She has long fair hair down to her knees."

'Of course I laughed. "You're mixing her up with the Valkyries," I said. "Lord, it would be an awkward business if you met that she-dragon in the flesh."

'But he was quite solemn about it, and declared that his waking picture of her was not in the least like his dreams. He rather agreed with my nonsense about the old schloss. He thought that she was probably some penniless grandee, living solitary in a moated grange, with nothing now to exercise her marvellous brain on, and eating her heart out with regret and shame. He drew so attractive a character of her that I began to think that Channell was in love with a being of his own creation, till he ended with, "But all the same she's utterly damnable. She must be, you know."

'After a fortnight I began to feel a different man. Dr Christoph thought that he had got on the track of the mischief, and certainly, with his deep massage and a few simple drugs, I had more internal comfort than I had known for three years. He was so pleased with my progress that he refused to treat me as an invalid. He encouraged me to take long walks into the hills, and presently he arranged for me to go out roebuck-shooting with some of the local junkers.

'I used to start before daybreak on the chilly November mornings and drive to the top of one of the ridges, where I would meet a collection of sportsmen and beaters, shepherded by a fellow in a green uniform. We lined out along the ridge, and the beaters, assisted by a marvellous collection of dogs, including the sporting dachshund, drove the roe towards us. It wasn't very cleverly managed, for the deer generally broke back, and it was chilly waiting in the first hours with a powdering of snow on the ground and the fir boughs heavy with frost crystals. But later, when the sun grew stronger, it was a very pleasant mode of spending a day. There was not much of a bag, but whenever a roe or a capercailzie fell all the guns would assemble and drink little glasses of *kirschwasser*. I had been lent a rifle, one of those appalling contraptions which are double-barrelled shot-guns and rifles in one, and to transpose from one form to the other requires a mathematical calculation. The rifle had a hair trigger too, and when I first used it I was nearly the death of a respectable Saxon peasant.

'We all ate our midday meal together and in the evening, before going home, we had coffee and cakes in one or other of the farms. The party was an odd mixture, big farmers and small squires, an hotel-keeper or two, a local doctor, and a couple of lawyers from the town. At first they were a little shy of me, but presently they thawed, and after the first day we were good friends. They spoke quite frankly about the War, in which every one of them had had a share, and with a great deal of dignity and good sense.

'I learned to walk in Sikkim, and the little Saxon hills seemed to me inconsiderable. But they were too much for most of the guns, and instead of going straight up or down a slope they always chose a circuit, which gave them an easy gradient. One evening, when we were separating as usual, the beaters taking a short cut and the guns a circuit, I felt that I wanted exercise, so I raced the beaters downhill, beat them soundly, and had the better part of an hour to wait for my companions, before we adjourned to the farm for refreshment. The beaters must have talked about my pace, for as we walked away one of the guns, a lawyer called Meissen, asked me why I was visiting Rosensee at a time of year when few foreigners came. I said I was staying with Dr Christoph.

' "Is he then a private friend of yours?" he asked.

'I told him No, that I had come to his kurhaus for treatment, being sick. His eyes expressed polite scepticism. He was not prepared to regard as an invalid a man who went down a hill like an avalanche.

'But, as we walked in the frosty dusk, he was led to speak of Dr Christoph, of whom he had no personal knowledge, and I learned how little honour a prophet may have in his own country. Rosensee scarcely knew him, except as a doctor who had an inexplicable attraction for foreign patients. Meissen was curious about his methods and the exact diseases in which he specialized. "Perhaps he may yet save me a journey to Homburg?" he laughed. "It is well to have a skilled physician at one's doorstep. The doctor is something of a hermit, and except for his patients does not appear to welcome his kind. Yet he is a good man, beyond doubt, and there are those who say that in the War he was a hero."

'This surprised me, for I could not imagine Dr Christoph in any fighting capacity, apart from the fact that he must have been too old. I thought that Meissen might refer to work in the base hospitals. But he was positive; Dr Christoph had been in the trenches; the limping leg was a war wound.

'I had had very little talk with the doctor, owing to my case being free from nervous complications. He would say a word to me morning and evening about my diet, and pass the time of day when we met, but it was not till the very eve of my departure that we had anything like a real conversation. He sent a message that he wanted to see me for not less than one hour, and he arrived with a batch of notes from which he delivered a kind of lecture on my case. Then I realized what an immense amount of care and solid thought he had expended on me. He had decided that his diagnosis was right—my rapid improvement suggested that—but it was necessary for some time to observe a simple regime, and to keep an eye on certain symptoms. So he took a sheet of note-paper from the table and in his small precise hand wrote down for me a few plain commandments.

'There was something about him, the honest eyes, the mouth which looked as if it had been often compressed in suffering, the air of grave goodwill, which I found curiously attractive. I wished that I had been a mental case like Channell, and had had more of his society. I detained him in talk, and he seemed not unwilling. By and by we drifted to the War and it turned out that Meissen was right.

'Dr Christoph had gone as medical officer in November '14 to the Ypres Salient with a Saxon regiment, and had spent the winter there. In '15 he had been in Champagne, and in the early months of '16 at Verdun, till he was invalided with rheumatic fever. That is to say, he had had about seventeen months of consecutive fighting in the worst areas with scarcely a holiday. A pretty good record for a frail little middle-aged man!

'His family was then at Stuttgart, his wife and one little boy. He took a long time to recover from the fever, and after that was put on home duty. "Till the War was almost over," he said, "almost over, but not quite. There was just time for me to go back to the front and get my foolish leg hurt." I must tell you that whenever he mentioned his war experience it was with a comical deprecating smile, as if he agreed with anyone who might think that gravity like his should have remained in bed.

'I assumed that this home duty was medical, until he said something about getting rusty in his professional work. Then it appeared that it had been some job connected with Intelligence. "I am reputed to have a little talent for mathematics," he said. "No. I am no mathematical scholar, but, if you understand me, I have a certain mathematical aptitude. My mind has always moved happily among numbers. Therefore I was set to construct and to interpret cyphers, a strange interlude in the noise of war. I sat in a little room and excluded the world, and for a little I was happy."

'He went on to speak of the *enclave* of peace in which he had found himself, and as I listened to his gentle monotonous voice, I had a sudden inspiration.

'I took a sheet of note-paper from the stand, scribbled the word *Reinmar* on it, and shoved it towards him. I had a notion, you see, that I might surprise him into helping Channell's researches.

'But it was I who got the big surprise. He stopped thunderstruck, as soon as his eye caught the word, blushed scarlet over every inch of face and bald forehead, seemed to have difficulty in swallowing, and then gasped. "How did you know?"

'I hadn't known, and now that I did, the knowledge left me speechless. This was the loathly opposite for which Channell and I had nursed our hatred. When I came out of my stupefaction I found that he had recovered his balance and was speaking slowly and distinctly, as if he were making a formal confession.

' "You were among my opponents . . . that interests me deeply . . . I often wondered . . . You beat me in the end. You are aware of that?"

'I nodded. "Only because you made a slip," I said.

' "Yes, I made a slip. I was to blame—very gravely to blame, for I let my private grief cloud my mind."

'He seemed to hesitate, as if he were loath to stir something very tragic in his memory.

' "I think I will tell you," he said at last. "I have often wished—it is a childish wish—to justify my failure to those who profited by it. My chiefs understood, of course, but my opponents could not. In that month when I failed I was in deep sorrow. I had a little son—his name was Reinmar— you remember that I took that name for my code signature?"

'His eyes were looking beyond me into some vision of the past.

' "He was, as you say, my mascot. He was all my family, and I adored him. But in those days food was not plentiful. We were no worse off than many million Germans, but the child was frail. In the last summer of the War he developed phthisis due to malnutrition, and in September he died. Then I failed my country, for with him some virtue seemed to depart from my mind. You see, my work was, so to speak, his also, as my name was his, and when he left me he took my power with him . . . So I stumbled. The rest is known to you."

'He sat staring beyond me, so small and lonely, that I could have howled. I remember putting my hand on his shoulder, and stammering some platitude about being sorry. We sat quite still for a minute or two, and then I remembered Channell. Channell must have poured his views of Reinmar into Dr Christoph's ear. I asked him if Channell knew.

'A flicker of a smile crossed his face.

' "Indeed no. And I will exact from you a promise never to breathe to him what I have told you. He is my patient, and I must first consider his case. At present he thinks that Reinmar is a wicked and beautiful lady whom he may some day meet. That is romance, and it is good for him to think so ... If he were told the truth, he would be pitiful, and in Herr Channell's condition it is important that he should not be vexed with such emotions as pity." '

Giulia Lazzari

FROM 'ASHENDEN'

W. SOMERSET MAUGHAM

◆——————◆

*Every reader of the 'Ashenden' collection has his favourite
episode. If the question were polled, I believe that 'The Hairless
Mexican' would probably receive the most votes, closely followed
by 'The Traitor' and 'Mr Harrington's Washing'.*

*My own vote, now, would go to 'Giulia Lazzari'. I say 'now',
because the test I have applied is that of time. This, I find, is
the episode that I most enjoy re-reading. The preliminary scenes
with R. are a perennial delight, and Madame Lazzari is so
vividly presented that you can almost see the pores of her skin.
It is an ugly story, but a highly satisfying one.*

◆——————◆

Ashenden was in the habit of asserting that he was never bored.
It was one of his notions that only such persons were as had
no resources in themselves and it was but the stupid that
depended on the outside world for their amusement. Ashenden
had no illusions about himself and such success in current
letters as had come to him had left his head unturned. He
distinguished acutely between fame and the notoriety that
rewards the author of a successful novel or a popular play;
and he was indifferent to this except in so far as it was attended
with tangible benefits. He was perfectly ready to take advantage
of his familiar name to get a better state-room in a ship than
he had paid for, and if a Customs-house officer passed his

luggage unopened because he had read his short stories
Ashenden was pleased to admit that the pursuit of literature
had its compensations. He sighed when eager young students
of the drama sought to discuss its technique with him, and
when gushing ladies tremulously whispered in his ear their
admiration of his books he often wished he was dead. But he
thought himself intelligent and so it was absurd that he should
be bored. It was a fact that he could talk with interest to
persons commonly thought so excruciatingly dull that their
fellows fled from them as though they owed them money.
It may be that here he was but indulging the professional
instinct that was seldom dormant in him; they, his raw
material, did not bore him any more than fossils bore the
geologist. And now he had everything that a reasonable man
could want for his entertainment. He had pleasant rooms in a
good hotel and Geneva is one of the most agreeable cities in
Europe to live in. He hired a boat and rowed on the lake or
hired a horse and trotted sedately, for in that neat and orderly
canton it is difficult to find a stretch of turf where you can
have a good gallop, along the macadamized roads in the
environs of the town. He wandered on foot about its old
streets, trying among those grey stone houses, so quiet and
dignified, to recapture the spirit of a past age. He read again
with delight Rousseau's *Confessions*, and for the second or
third time tried in vain to get on with *La Nouvelle Héloïse*.
He wrote. He knew few people, for it was his business to keep
in the background, but he had picked up a chatting acquaintance with several persons living in his hotel and he was not
lonely. His life was sufficiently filled, it was varied, and when
he had nothing else to do he could enjoy his own reflections;
it was absurd to think that under these circumstances he could
possibly be bored, and yet, like a little lonely cloud in the sky,

he did see in the offing the possibility of boredom. There is a story that Louis XIV, having summoned a courtier to attend him on a ceremonial occasion, found himself ready to go as the courtier appeared; he turned to him and with icy majesty said, *J'ai failli attendre*, of which the only translation I can give, but a poor one, is, I have but just escaped waiting; so Ashenden might have admitted that he now but just escaped being bored.

It might be, he mused, as he rode along the lake on a dappled horse with a great rump and a short neck, like one of those prancing steeds that you see in old pictures, but this horse never pranced and he needed a firm jab with the spur to break even into a smart trot—it might be, he mused, that the great chiefs of the secret service in their London offices, their hands on the throttle of this great machine, led a life full of excitement; they moved their pieces here and there, they saw the pattern woven by the multitudinous threads (Ashenden was lavish with his metaphors), they made a picture out of the various pieces of the jigsaw puzzle; but it must be confessed that for the small fry like himself to be a member of the secret service was not as adventurous an affair as the public thought. Ashenden's official existence was as orderly and monotonous as a city clerk's. He saw his spies at stated intervals and paid them their wages; when he could get hold of a new one he engaged him, gave him his instructions and sent him off to Germany; he waited for the information that came through and despatched it; he went into France once a week to confer with his colleague over the frontier and to receive his orders from London; he visited the market-place on market-day to get any message the old butter-woman had brought him from the other side of the lake; he kept his eyes and ears open; and he wrote long reports which he was convinced no one read, till having inadvertently slipped a jest into one of them he received a sharp reproof for his levity. The work he was doing was evidently necessary, but it could not be called anything but monotonous. At one moment for something better to do he had considered the possibility of a flirtation with the Baroness von Higgins. He was confident now that she was an agent in the service of the Austrian Government and he looked forward to a certain entertainment in the duel he foresaw. It would be amusing to set his wits against hers. He was quite aware that she would lay snares for him and to avoid them would give him something to keep his mind from rusting. He found her not unwilling to play the game. She wrote him gushing little notes when he sent her flowers. She went for a row with him on the lake and letting her long white hand drag through the water talked of Love and hinted at a Broken Heart. They dined together and went to see a performance, in French and in prose, of *Romeo and Juliet*. Ashenden had not made up his mind how far he was prepared to go when he received a sharp note from R. to ask him what he was playing at: information 'had come to hand' that he (Ashenden) was much in the society of a woman calling herself the Baroness de Higgins, who was known to be an agent of the Central Powers and it was most undesirable that he should be on any terms with her but those of frigid courtesy. Ashenden shrugged his shoulders. R. did not think him as clever as he thought himself. But he was interested to discover, what he had not known before, that there was someone in Geneva part of whose duties at all events was to keep an eye on him. There was evidently someone who had orders to see that he did not neglect his work or get into mischief. Ashenden was not a little amused. What a shrewd, unscrupulous old thing was R.! He took no risks; he trusted nobody; he made use of his instruments,

but, high or low, had no opinion of them. Ashenden looked
about to see whether he could spot the person who had told
R. what he was doing. He wondered if it was one of the waiters
in the hotel. He knew that R. had a great belief in waiters;
they had the chance of seeing so much and could so easily
get into places where information was lying about to be picked
up. He even wondered whether R. had got his news from the
Baroness herself; it would not be so strange if after all she was
employed by the secret service of one of the Allied nations.
Ashenden continued to be polite to the Baroness, but ceased
to be attentive.

He turned his horse and trotted gently back to Geneva. An
ostler from the riding-stables was waiting at the hotel door
and slipping out of the saddle Ashenden went into the hotel.
At the desk the porter handed him a telegram. It was to the
following effect:

*Aunt Maggie not at all well. Staying at Hôtel Lotti, Paris.
If possible please go and see her. Raymond.*

Raymond was one of R.'s facetious *noms de guerre*, and since
Ashenden was not so fortunate as to possess an Aunt Maggie
he concluded that this was an order to go to Paris. It had
always seemed to Ashenden that R. had spent much of his
spare time in reading detective fiction and especially when he
was in a good humour he found a fantastic pleasure in aping
the style of the shilling shocker. If R. was in a good humour it
meant that he was about to bring off a coup, for when he had
brought one off he was filled with depression and then vented
his spleen on his subordinates.

Ashenden, leaving his telegram with deliberate carelessness
on the desk, asked at what time the express left for Paris. He
glanced at the clock to see whether he had time to get to the

Consulate before it closed and secure his visa. When he went upstairs to fetch his passport the porter, just as the lift doors were closed, called him.

'*Monsieur* has forgotten his telegram,' he said.

'How stupid of me,' said Ashenden.

Now Ashenden knew that if an Austrian baroness by any chance wondered why he had so suddenly gone to Paris she would discover that it was owing to the indisposition of a female relative. In those troublous times of war it was just as well that everything should be clear and above board. He was known at the French Consulate and so lost little time there. He had told the porter to get him a ticket and on his return to the hotel bathed and changed. He was not a little excited at the prospect of this unexpected jaunt. He liked the journey. He slept well in a sleeping-car and was not disturbed if a sudden jolt wakened him; it was pleasant to lie a while smoking a cigarette and to feel oneself in one's little cabin so enchantingly alone; the rhythmical sound as the wheels rattled over the points was an agreeable background to the pattern of one's reflections, and to speed through the open country and the night made one feel like a star speeding through space. And at the end of the journey was the unknown.

When Ashenden arrived in Paris it was chilly and a light rain was falling; he felt unshaved and he wanted a bath and clean linen; but he was in excellent spirits. He telephoned from the station to R. and asked how Aunt Maggie was.

'I'm glad to see that your affection for her was great enough to allow you to waste no time in getting here,' answered R., with the ghost of a chuckle in his voice. 'She's very low, but I'm sure it'll do her good to see you.'

Ashenden reflected that this was the mistake the amateur humorist, as opposed to the professional, so often made; when he made a joke he harped on it. The relations of the joker to his joke should be as quick and desultory as those of a bee to its flower. He should make his joke and pass on. There is of course no harm if, like the bee approaching the flower, he buzzes a little; for it is just as well to announce to a thick-headed world that a joke is intended. But Ashenden, unlike most professional humorists, had a kindly tolerance for other people's humour and now he answered R. on his own lines.

'When would she like to see me, do you think?' he asked. 'Give her my love, won't you?'

Now R. quite distinctly chuckled. Ashenden sighed.

'She'll want to titivate a little before you come, I expect. You know what she is, she likes to make the best of herself. Shall we say half past ten, and then when you've had a talk to her we might go out and lunch together somewhere.'

'All right,' said Ashenden. 'I'll come to the Lotti at ten-thirty.'

When Ashenden, clean and refreshed, reached the hotel an orderly whom he recognized met him in the hall and took him up to R.'s apartment. He opened the door and showed Ashenden in. R. was standing with his back to a bright log fire dictating to his secretary.

'Sit down,' said R. and went on with his dictation.

It was a nicely furnished sitting-room and a bunch of roses in a bowl gave the impression of a woman's hand. On a large table was a litter of papers. R. looked older than when last Ashenden had seen him. His thin yellow face was more lined and his hair was greyer. The work was telling on him. He did not spare himself. He was up at seven every morning and he worked late into the night. His uniform was spick and span, but he wore it shabbily.

'That'll do,' he said. 'Take all this stuff away and get on

with the typing. I'll sign before I go out to lunch.' Then he turned to the orderly. 'I don't want to be disturbed.'

The secretary, a second-lieutenant in the thirties, obviously a civilian with a temporary commission, gathered up a mass of papers and left the room. As the orderly was following, R. said:

'Wait outside. If I want you I'll call.'

'Very good, sir.'

When they were alone R. turned to Ashenden with what for him was cordiality.

'Have a nice journey up?'

'Yes, sir.'

'What do you think of this?' he asked, looking round the room. 'Not bad, is it? I never see why one shouldn't do what one can to mitigate the hardships of war.'

While he was idly chatting R. gazed at Ashenden with a singular fixity. The stare of those pale eyes of his, too closely set together, gave you the impression that he looked at your naked brain and had a very poor opinion of what he saw there. R. in rare moments of expansion made no secret of the fact that he looked upon his fellow-men as fools or knaves. That was one of the obstacles he had to contend with in his calling. On the whole he preferred them knaves; you knew then what you were up against and could take steps accordingly. He was a professional soldier and had spent his career in India and the Colonies. At the outbreak of the war he was stationed in Jamaica and someone in the War Office who had had dealings with him, remembering him, brought him over and put him in the Intelligence Department. His astuteness was so great that he very soon occupied an important post. He had an immense energy and a gift for organization, no scruples, but resource, courage and determination. He had perhaps but one

48

weakness. Throughout his life he had never come in contact with persons, especially women, of any social consequence; the only women he had ever known were the wives of his brother officers, the wives of government officials and of business men; and when, coming to London at the beginning of the war, his work brought him into contact with brilliant, beautiful and distinguished women he was unduly dazzled. They made him feel shy, but he cultivated their society; he became quite a lady's man, and to Ashenden, who knew more about him than R. suspected, that bowl of roses told a story.

Ashenden knew that R. had not sent for him to talk about the weather and the crops, and wondered when he was coming to the point. He did not wonder long.

'You've been doing pretty well in Geneva,' he said.

'I'm glad you think that, sir,' replied Ashenden.

Suddenly R. looked very cold and stern. He had done with idle talk.

'I've got a job for you,' he said.

Ashenden made no reply, but he felt a happy little flutter somewhere about the pit of his stomach.

'Have you ever heard of Chandra Lal?'

'No, sir.'

A frown of impatience for an instant darkened the Colonel's brow. He expected his subordinates to know everything he wished them to know.

'Where have you been living all these years?'

'At 36 Chesterfield Street, Mayfair,' returned Ashenden.

The shadow of a smile crossed R.'s yellow face. The somewhat impertinent reply was after his own sardonic heart. He went over to the big table and opened a despatch-case that lay upon it. He took out a photograph and handed it to Ashenden.

'That's him.'

To Ashenden, unused to Oriental faces, it looked like any of a hundred Indians that he had seen. It might have been the photograph of one or other of the rajahs who come periodically to England and are portrayed in the illustrated papers. It showed a fat-faced, swarthy man, with full lips and a fleshy nose; his hair was black, thick and straight, and his very large eyes even in the photograph were liquid and cow-like. He looked ill-at-ease in European clothes.

'Here he is in native dress,' said R., giving Ashenden another photograph.

This was full-length, whereas the first had shown only the head and shoulders, and it had evidently been taken some years earlier. He was thinner and his great, serious eyes seemed to devour his face. It was done by a native photographer in Calcutta and the surroundings were naïvely grotesque. Chandra Lal stood against a background on which had been painted a pensive palm tree and a view of the sea. One hand rested on a heavily carved table on which was a rubber-plant in a flower-pot. But in his turban and long, pale tunic he was not without dignity.

'What d'you think of him?' asked R.

'I should have said he was a man not without personality. There is a certain force there.'

'Here's his dossier. Read it, will you?'

R. gave Ashenden a couple of typewritten pages and Ashenden sat down. R. put on his spectacles and began to read the letters that awaited his signature. Ashenden skimmed the report and then read it a second time more attentively. It appeared that Chandra Lal was a dangerous agitator. He was a lawyer by profession, but had taken up politics and was bitterly hostile to the British rule in India. He was a partisan of armed force and had been on more than one occasion responsible for riots in which life had been lost. He was once arrested, tried and sentenced to two years' imprisonment; but he was at liberty at the beginning of the war and seizing his opportunity began to foment active rebellion. He was at the heart of plots to embarrass the British in India and so prevent them from transferring troops to the seat of war and with the help of immense sums given to him by German agents he was able to cause a great deal of trouble. He was concerned in two or three bomb outrages which, though beyond killing a few innocent bystanders they did little harm, yet shook the nerves of the public and so damaged its morale. He evaded all attempts to arrest him, his activity was formidable, he was here and there; but the police could never lay hands on him, and they only learned that he had been in some city when, having done his work, he had left it. At last a high reward was offered for his arrest on a charge of murder, but he escaped the country, got to America, from there went to Sweden and eventually reached Berlin. Here he busied himself with schemes to create disaffection among the native troops that had been brought to Europe. All this was narrated dryly, without comment or explanation, but from the very frigidity of the narrative you got a sense of mystery and adventure, of hairbreadth escapes and dangers dangerously encountered. The report ended as follows:

'C. has a wife in India and two children. He is not known to have anything to do with women. He neither drinks nor smokes. He is said to be honest. Considerable sums of money have passed through his hands and there has never been any question as to his not having made a proper (!) use of them. He has undoubted courage and is a hard worker. He is said to pride himself on keeping his word.'

Ashenden returned the document to R.

'Well?'

'A fanatic.' Ashenden thought there was about the man something rather romantic and attractive, but he knew that R. did not want any nonsense of that sort from him. 'He looks like a very dangerous fellow.'

'He is the most dangerous conspirator in or out of India. He's done more harm than all the rest of them put together. You know that there's a gang of these Indians in Berlin; well, he's the brains of it. If he could be got out of the way I could afford to ignore the others; he's the only one who has any guts. I've been trying to catch him for a year, I thought there wasn't a hope; but now at last I've got a chance and, by God, I'm going to take it.'

'And what'll you do then?'

R. chuckled grimly.

'Shoot him and shoot him damn quick.'

Ashenden did not answer. R. walked once or twice across the small room and then, again with his back to the fire, faced Ashenden. His thin mouth was twisted by a sarcastic smile.

'Did you notice at the end of that report I gave you it said he wasn't known to have anything to do with women? Well, that *was* true, but it isn't any longer. The damned fool has fallen in love.'

R. stepped over to his despatch-case and took out a bundle tied up with pale blue ribbon.

'Look, here are his love-letters. You're a novelist, it might amuse you to read them. In fact you should read them, it will help you to deal with the situation. Take them away with you.'

R. flung the neat little bundle back into the despatch-case.

'One wonders how an able man like that can allow himself to get besotted over a woman. It was the last thing I ever expected of him.'

52

Ashenden's eyes travelled to the bowl of beautiful roses that stood on the table, but he said nothing. R., who missed little, saw the glance and his look suddenly darkened. Ashenden knew that he felt like asking him what the devil he was staring at. At that moment R. had no friendly feelings towards his subordinate, but he made no remark. He went back to the subject in hand.

'Anyhow that's neither here nor there. Chandra has fallen madly in love with a woman called Giulia Lazzari. He's crazy about her.'

'Do you know how he picked her up?'

'Of course I do. She's a dancer, and she does Spanish dances, but she happens to be an Italian. For stage purposes she calls herself La Malagueña. You know the kind of thing. Popular Spanish music and a mantilla, a fan and a high comb. She's been dancing all over Europe for the last ten years.'

'Is she any good?'

'No, rotten. She's been in the provinces in England and she's had a few engagements in London. She never got more than ten pounds a week. Chandra met her in Berlin in a Tingel-tangel, you know what that is, a cheap sort of music-hall. I take it that on the Continent she looked upon her dancing chiefly as a means to enhance her value as a prostitute.'

'How did she get to Berlin during the war?'

'She's been married to a Spaniard at one time; I think she still is though they don't live together, and she travelled on a Spanish passport. It appears Chandra made a dead set for her.' R. took up the Indian's photograph again and looked at it thoughtfully. 'You wouldn't have thought there was anything very attractive in that greasy little nigger. God, how they run to fat! The fact remains that she fell very nearly as much in love with him as he did with her. I've got her letters too, only copies, of course, he's got the originals and I dare say he keeps them tied up in pink ribbon. She's mad about him. I'm not a literary man, but I think I know when a thing rings true; anyhow you'll be reading them, and you can tell me what you think. And then people say there's no such thing as love at first sight.'

R. smiled with faint irony. He was certainly in a good humour this morning.

'But how did you get hold of all these letters?'

'How did I get hold of them? How do you imagine? Owing to her Italian nationality Giulia Lazzari was eventually expelled from Germany. She was put over the Dutch frontier. Having an engagement to dance in England she was granted a visa and'—R. looked up a date among the papers—'and on the twenty-fourth of October last sailed from Rotterdam to Harwich. Since then she has danced in London, Birmingham, Portsmouth and other places. She was arrested a fortnight ago at Hull.'

'What for?'

'Espionage. She was transferred to London and I went to see her myself at Holloway.'

Ashenden and R. looked at one another for a moment without speaking and it may be that each was trying his hardest to read the other's thoughts. Ashenden was wondering where the truth in all this lay and R. wondered how much of it he could advantageously tell him.

'How did you get on to her?'

'I thought it odd that the Germans should allow her to dance quite quietly in Berlin for weeks and then for no particular reason decide to put her out of the country. It would be a good introduction for espionage. And a dancer who was not too careful of her virtue might make opportunities of learning things that it would be worth somebody's while in Berlin to pay a good price for. I thought it might be as well to let her come to England and see what she was up to. I kept track of her. I discovered that she was sending letters to an address in Holland two or three times a week and two or three times a week was receiving answers from Holland. Hers were written in a queer mixture of French, German and English; she speaks English a little and French quite well, but the answers were written entirely in English; it was good English, but not an Englishman's English, flowery and rather grandiloquent; I wondered who was writing them. They seemed to be just ordinary love-letters, but they were by way of being rather hot stuff. It was plain enough that they were coming from Germany and the writer was neither English, French nor German. Why did he write in English? The only foreigners who know English better than any continental language are Orientals, and not Turks or Egyptians either; they know French. A Jap would write English and so would an Indian. I came to the conclusion that Giulia's lover was one of that gang of Indians that were making trouble for us in Berlin. I had no idea it was Chandra Lal till I found the photograph.'

'How did you get that?'

'She carried it about with her. It was a pretty good bit of work, that. She kept it locked up in her trunk, with a lot of theatrical photographs, of comic singers and clowns and acrobats; it might easily have passed for the picture of some music-hall artist in his stage dress. In fact, later, when she was arrested and asked who the photograph represented she said she didn't know, it was an Indian conjuror who had given it her and she had no idea what his name was. Anyhow I put a very smart lad on the job and he thought it queer that it should be the only photograph in the lot that came from Calcutta. He noticed that there was a number on the back, and he took it, the number, I mean; of course the photograph was replaced in the box.'

'By the way, just as a matter of interest how did your very smart lad get at the photograph at all?'

R.'s eyes twinkled.

'That's none of your business. But I don't mind telling you that he was a good-looking boy. Anyhow it's of no consequence. When we got the number of the photograph we cabled to Calcutta and in a little while I received the grateful news that the object of Giulia's affections was no less a person than the incorruptible Chandra Lal. Then I thought it my duty to have Giulia watched a little more carefully. She seemed to have a sneaking fondness for naval officers. I couldn't exactly blame her for that; they are attractive, but it is unwise for ladies of easy virtue and doubtful nationality to cultivate their society in war-time. Presently I got a very pretty little body of evidence against her.'

'How was she getting her stuff through?'

'She wasn't getting it through. She wasn't trying to. The Germans had turned her out quite genuinely; she wasn't working for them, she was working for Chandra. After her engagement was through in England she was planning to go to Holland again and meet him. She wasn't very clever at the work; she was nervous, but it looked easy; no one seemed to bother about her, it grew rather exciting; she was getting all sorts of interesting information without any risk. In one of her letters she said: "I have so much to tell you, *mon petit chou* darling, and what you will be *extrêmement intéressé* to know", and she underlined the French words.'

R. paused and rubbed his hands together. His tired face bore a look of devilish enjoyment of his own cunning.

'It was espionage made easy. Of course I didn't care a damn about her, it was him I was after. Well, as soon as I'd got the goods on her I arrested her. I had enough evidence to convict a regiment of spies.'

R. put his hands in his pockets and his pale lips twisted to a smile that was almost a grimace.

'Holloway's not a very cheerful place, you know.'

'I imagine no prison is,' remarked Ashenden.

'I left her to stew in her own juice for a week before I went to see her. She was in a very pretty state of nerves by then. The wardress told me she'd been in violent hysterics most of the time. I must say she looked like the devil.'

'Is she handsome?'

'You'll see for yourself. She's not my type. I dare say she's better when she's made up and that kind of thing. I talked to her like a Dutch uncle. I put the fear of God into her. I told her she'd get ten years. I think I scared her, I know I tried to. Of course she denied everything, but the proofs were there, I assured her she hadn't got a chance. I spent three hours with her. She went all to pieces and at last she confessed everything. Then I told her that I'd let her go scot-free if she'd get Chandra to come to France. She absolutely refused, she said she'd rather die; she was very hysterical and tiresome, but I let her rave. I told her to think it over and said I'd see her in a day or two and we'd have another talk about it. In point of fact I left her for a week. She'd evidently had time to reflect, because when I came again she asked me quite calmly what it was exactly that I proposed. She'd been in a gaol a fortnight then and I expect she'd had about enough of it. I put it to her as plainly as I could and she accepted.'

'I don't think I quite understand,' said Ashenden.

'Don't you? I should have thought it was clear to the meanest intelligence. If she can get Chandra to cross the Swiss frontier and come into France she's to go free, either to Spain or to South America, with her passage paid.'

'And how the devil is she to get Chandra to do that?'

'He's madly in love with her. He's longing to see her. His letters are almost crazy. She's written to him to say that she can't get a visa to Holland (I told you she was to join him there when her tour was over), but she can get one for Switzerland. That's a neutral country and he's safe there. He jumped at the chance. They've arranged to meet at Lausanne.'

'Yes.'

'When he reaches Lausanne he'll get a letter from her to say that the French authorities won't let her cross the frontier and that she's going to Thonon, which is just on the other side of the lake from Lausanne, in France, and she's going to ask him to come there.'

'What makes you think he will?'

R. paused for an instant. He looked at Ashenden with a pleasant expression.

'She must make him if she doesn't want to go to penal servitude for ten years.'

'I see.'

'She's arriving from England this evening in custody and I should like you to take her down to Thonon by the night train.'

'Me?' said Ashenden.

'Yes, I thought it the sort of job you could manage very well. Presumably you know more about human nature than most people. It'll be a pleasant change for you to spend a week or two at Thonon. I believe it's a pretty little place, fashionable too—in peace-time. You might take the baths there.'

'And what do you expect me to do when I get the lady down to Thonon?'

'I leave you a free hand. I've made a few notes that may be useful to you. I'll read them to you, shall I?'

Ashenden listened attentively. R.'s plan was simple and explicit. Ashenden could not but feel unwilling admiration for the brain that had so neatly devised it.

Presently R. suggested that they should have luncheon and he asked Ashenden to take him to some place where they could see smart people. It amused Ashenden to see R., so sharp, sure of himself and alert in his office, seized as he walked into the restaurant with shyness. He talked a little too loud in order to show that he was at his ease and made himself somewhat unnecessarily at home. You saw in his manner the shabby and commonplace life he had led till the hazards of war raised him to a position of consequence. He was glad to be in that fashionable restaurant cheek by jowl with persons who bore great or distinguished names, but he felt like a school-boy in his first top-hat, and he quailed before the steely eye of the *maître d'hôtel*. His quick glance darted here and there and his sallow face beamed with a self-satisfaction of which he was slightly ashamed. Ashenden drew his attention to an ugly woman in black, with a lovely figure, wearing a long row of pearls.

'That is Madame de Brides. She is the mistress of the Grand Duke Theodore. She's probably one of the most influential women in Europe, she's certainly one of the cleverest.'

R.'s clever eyes rested on her and he flushed a little.

'By George, this is life,' he said.

Ashenden watched him curiously. Luxury is dangerous to people who have never known it and to whom its temptations are held out too suddenly. R., that shrewd, cynical man, was captivated by the vulgar glamour and the shoddy brilliance of the scene before him. Just as the advantage of culture is that it enables you to talk nonsense with distinction, so the habit of luxury allows you to regard its frills and furbelows with a proper contumely.

But when they had eaten their luncheon and were drinking their coffee Ashenden, seeing that R. was mellowed by the good meal and his surroundings, went back to the subject that was in his thoughts.

'That Indian fellow must be a rather remarkable chap,' he said.

'He's got brains, of course.'

'One can't help being impressed by a man who had the courage to take on almost single-handed the whole British power in India.'

'I wouldn't get sentimental about him if I were you. He's nothing but a dangerous criminal.'

'I don't suppose he'd use bombs if he could command a few batteries and half a dozen battalions. He uses what weapons he can. You can hardly blame him for that. After all, he's aiming at nothing for himself, is he? He's aiming at freedom for his country. On the face of it it looks as though he were justified in his actions.'

But R. had no notion of what Ashenden was talking.

'That's very far-fetched and morbid,' he said. 'We can't go into all that. Our job is to get him and when we've got him to shoot him.'

'Of course. He's declared war and he must take his chance. I shall carry out your instructions, that's what I'm here for, but I see no harm in realizing that there's something to be admired and respected in him.'

R. was once more the cool and astute judge of his fellows.

'I've not yet made up my mind whether the best men for this kind of job are those who do it with passion or those who keep their heads. Some of them are filled with hatred for the people we're up against and when we down them it gives them a sort of satisfaction like satisfying a personal grudge. Of course they're very keen on their work. You're different, aren't you? You look at it like a game of chess and you don't seem to have any feeling one way or the other. I can't quite make it out. Of course for some sort of jobs it's just what one wants.'

Ashenden did not answer. He called for the bill and walked back with R. to the hotel.

The train started at eight. When he had disposed of his bag Ashenden walked along the platform. He found the carriage in which Giulia Lazzari was, but she sat in a corner, looking away from the light, so that he could not see her face. She was in charge of two detectives who had taken her over from English police at Boulogne. One of them worked with Ashenden on the French side of the Lake Geneva and as Ashenden came up he nodded to him.

'I've asked the lady if she will dine in the restaurant-car, but she prefers to have dinner in the carriage, so I've ordered a basket. Is that quite correct?'

'Quite,' said Ashenden.

'My companion and I will go into the diner in turn so that she will not remain alone.'

'That is very considerate of you. I will come along when we've started and have a chat with her.'

'She's not disposed to be very talkative,' said the detective.

'One could hardly expect it,' replied Ashenden.

He walked on to get his ticket for the second service and then returned to his own carriage. Giulia Lazzari was just finishing her meal when he went back to her. From a glance at the basket he judged that she had not eaten with too poor an appetite. The detective who was guarding her opened the door when Ashenden appeared and at Ashenden's suggestion left them alone.

Giulia Lazzari gave him a sullen look.

'I hope you've had what you wanted for dinner,' he said as he sat down in front of her.

She bowed slightly, but did not speak. He took out his case.

'Will you have a cigarette?'

She gave him a glance, seemed to hesitate, and then, still without a word, took one. He struck a match and, lighting it, looked at her. He was surprised. For some reason he had expected her to be fair, perhaps from some notion that an Oriental would be more likely to fall for a blonde; but she was almost swarthy. Her hair was hidden by a close-fitting hat, but her eyes were coal-black. She was far from young, she might have been thirty-five, and her skin was lined and sallow. She had at the moment no make-up on and she looked haggard. There was nothing beautiful about her but her magnificent eyes. She was big, and Ashenden thought she must be too big to dance gracefully; it might be that in Spanish costume she was a bold and flaunting figure, but there in the train, shabbily dressed, there was nothing to explain the Indian's infatuation. She gave Ashenden a long, appraising stare. She wondered evidently what sort of man he was. She blew a cloud of smoke through her nostrils and gave it a glance, then looked back at Ashenden. He could see that her sullenness was only a mask, she was nervous and frightened. She spoke in French with an Italian accent.

'Who are you?'

'My name would mean nothing to you, *madame*. I am going to Thonon. I have taken a room for you at the Hôtel de la Place. It is the only one open now. I think you will find it quite comfortable.'

'Ah, it is you the Colonel spoke to me of. You are my gaoler.'

'Only as a matter of form. I shall not intrude upon you.'

'All the same you are my gaoler.'

'I hope not for very long. I have in my pocket your passport with all the formalities completed to permit you to go to Spain.'

She threw herself back into the corner of the carriage. White, with those great black eyes, in the poor light, her face was suddenly a mask of despair.

'It's infamous. Oh, I think I could die happy if I could only kill that old Colonel. He has no heart. I'm so unhappy.'

'I am afraid you have got yourself into a very unfortunate situation. Did you not know that espionage was a dangerous game?'

'I never sold any of the secrets. I did no harm.'

'Surely only because you had no opportunity. I understand that you signed a full confession.'

Ashenden spoke to her as amiably as he could, a little as though he were talking to a sick person, and there was no harshness in his voice.

'Oh, yes, I made a fool of myself. I wrote the letter the Colonel said I was to write. Why isn't that enough? What is to happen to me if he does not answer? I cannot force him to come if he does not want to.'

'He has answered,' said Ashenden. 'I have the answer with me.'

She gave a gasp and her voice broke.

'Oh, show it to me, I beseech you to let me see it.'

'I have no objection to doing that. But you must return it to me.'

He took Chandra's letter from his pocket and gave it to her. She snatched it from his hand. She devoured it with her eyes, there were eight pages of it, and as she read the tears streamed down her cheeks. Between her sobs she gave little exclamations of love, calling the writer by pet names French and Italian. This was the letter that Chandra had written in reply to hers telling him, on R.'s instructions, that she would meet him in Switzerland. He was mad with joy at the prospect. He told her in passionate phrases how long the time had seemed to him since they were parted, and how he had yearned for her, and now that he was to see her again so soon he did not know how he was going to bear his impatience. She finished it and let it drop to the floor.

'You can see he loves me, can't you? There's no doubt about that. I know something about it, believe me.'

'Do you really love him?' asked Ashenden.

'He's the only man who's ever been kind to me. It's not very gay, the life one leads in these music-halls, all over Europe, never resting, and men—they are not much, the men who haunt those places. At first I thought he was just like the rest of them.'

Ashenden picked up the letter and replaced it in his pocket-book.

'A telegram was sent in your name to the address in Holland to say that you would be at the Hotel Gibbons at Lausanne on the 14th.'

'That is to-morrow.'

'Yes.'

She threw up her head and her eyes flashed.

'Oh, it is an infamous thing that you are forcing me to do. It is shameful.'

'You are not obliged to do it,' said Ashenden.

'And if I don't?'

'I'm afraid you must take the consequences.'

'I can't go to prison,' she cried out suddenly, 'I can't, I

can't; I have such a short time before me; he said ten years.
Is it possible I could be sentenced to ten years?'

'If the Colonel told you so it is very possible.'

'Oh, I know him. That cruel face. He would have no mercy.
And what should I be in ten years? Oh, no no.'

At that moment the train stopped at a station and the detective waiting in the corridor tapped on the window. Ashenden
opened the door and the man gave him a picture-postcard.
It was a dull little view of Pontarlier, the frontier station
between France and Switzerland, and showed a dusty *place*
with a statue in the middle and a few plane-trees. Ashenden
handed her a pencil.

'Will you write this postcard to your lover. It will be posted
at Pontarlier. Address it to the hotel at Lausanne.'

She gave him a glance, but without answering took it and
wrote as he directed.

'Now on the other side write: "Delayed at frontier but
everything all right. Wait at Lausanne." Then add whatever
you like, *tendresses*, if you like.'

He took the postcard from her, read it to see that she had
done as he directed and then reached for his hat.

'Well, I shall leave you now, I hope you will have a sleep.
I will fetch you in the morning when we arrive at Thonon.'

The second detective had now returned from his dinner and
as Ashenden came out of the carriage the two men went in.
Giulia Lazzari huddled back into her corner. Ashenden gave
the postcard to an agent who was waiting to take it to Pontarlier
and then made his way along the crowded train to his sleeping-
car.

It was bright and sunny, though cold, next morning when
they reached their destination. Ashenden, having given his
bags to a porter, walked along the platform to where Giulia

Lazzari and the two detectives were standing. Ashenden nodded to them.

'Well, good morning. You need not trouble to wait.'

They touched their hats, gave a word of farewell to the woman, and walked away.

'Where are they going?' she asked.

'Off. You will not be bothered with them any more.'

'Am I in your custody then?'

'You're in nobody's custody. I'm going to permit myself to take you to your hotel and then I shall leave you. You must try to get a good rest.'

Ashenden's porter took her hand-luggage and she gave him the ticket for her trunk. They walked out of the station. A cab was waiting for them and Ashenden begged her to get in. It was a longish drive to the hotel and now and then Ashenden felt that she gave him a sidelong glance. She was perplexed. He sat without a word. When they reached the hotel the proprietor—it was a small hotel, prettily situated at the corner of a little promenade and it had a charming view—showed them the room that had been prepared for Madame Lazzari. Ashenden turned to him.

'That'll do very nicely, I think. I shall come down in a minute.'

The proprietor bowed and withdrew.

'I shall do my best to see that you are comfortable, *madame*,' said Ashenden. 'You are here absolutely your own mistress and you may order pretty well anything you like. To the proprietor you are just a guest of the hotel like any other. You are absolutely free.'

'Free to go out?' she asked quickly.

'Of course.'

'With a policeman on either side of me, I suppose.'

66

'Not at all. You are as free in the hotel as though you were in your own house and you are free to go out and come in when you choose. I should like an assurance from you that you will not write letters without my knowledge or attempt to leave Thonon without my permission.'

She gave Ashenden a long stare. She could not make it out at all. She looked as though she thought it a dream.

'I am in a position that forces me to give you any assurance you ask. I give you my word of honour that I will not write a letter without showing it to you or attempt to leave this place.'

'Thank you. Now I will leave you. I will do myself the pleasure of coming to see you to-morrow morning.'

Ashenden nodded and went out. He stopped for five minutes at the police-station to see that everything was in order and then took the cab up the hill to a little secluded house on the outskirts of the town at which on his periodical visits to this place he stayed. It was pleasant to have a bath and a shave and get into slippers. He felt lazy and spent the rest of the morning reading a novel.

Soon after dark, for even at Thonon, though it was in France, it was thought desirable to attract attention to Ashenden as little as possible, an agent from the police-station came to see him. His name was Felix. He was a little dark Frenchman with sharp eyes and an unshaven chin, dressed in a shabby grey suit and rather down at heel, so that he looked like a lawyer's clerk out of work. Ashenden offered him a glass of wine and they sat down by the fire.

'Well, your lady lost no time,' he said. 'Within a quarter of an hour of her arrival she was out of the hotel with a bundle of clothes and trinkets that she sold in a shop near the market. When the afternoon boat came in she went down to the quay and bought a ticket to Evian.'

Evian, it should be explained, was the next place along the lake in France, and from there, crossing over, the boat went to Switzerland.

'Of course she hadn't a passport, so permission to embark was denied her.'

'How did she explain that she had no passport?'

'She said she'd forgotten it. She said she had an appointment to see friends in Evian and tried to persuade the official in charge to let her go. She attempted to slip a hundred francs into his hand.'

'She must be a stupider woman than I thought,' said Ashenden.

But when next day he went about eleven in the morning to see her he made no reference to her attempt to escape. She had had time to arrange herself, and now, her hair elaborately done, her lips and cheeks painted, she looked less haggard than when he had first seen her.

'I've brought you some books,' said Ashenden. 'I'm afraid the time hangs heavy on your hands.'

'What does that matter to you?'

'I have no wish that you should suffer anything that can be avoided. Anyhow, I will leave them and you can read them or not as you choose.'

'If you only knew how I hated you.'

'It would doubtless make me very uncomfortable. But I really don't know why you should. I am only doing what I have been ordered to do.'

'What do you want of me now? I do not suppose you have come only to ask after my health.'

Ashenden smiled.

'I want you to write a letter to your lover telling him that owing to some irregularity in your passport the Swiss authorities would not let you cross the frontier, so you have come here where it is very nice and quiet, so quiet that one can hardly realize there is a war, and you propose that Chandra should join you.'

'Do you think he is a fool? He will refuse.'

'Then you must do your best to persuade him.'

She looked at Ashenden a long time before she answered. He suspected that she was debating within herself whether by writing the letter and so seeming docile she could not gain time.

'Well, dictate and I will write what you say.'

'I should prefer you to put it in your own words.'

'Give me half an hour and the letter shall be ready.'

'I will wait here,' said Ashenden.

'Why?'

'Because I prefer to.'

Her eyes flashed angrily, but controlling herself she said nothing. On the chest of drawers were writing materials. She sat down at the dressing-table and began to write. When she handed Ashenden the letter he saw that even through her rouge she was very pale. It was the letter of a person not much used to expressing herself by means of pen and ink, but it was well enough, and when towards the end, starting to say how much she loved the man, she had been carried away and wrote with all her heart, it had really a certain passion.

'Now add: the man who is bringing this is Swiss, you can trust him absolutely. I didn't want the censor to see it.'

She hesitated an instant, but then wrote as he directed.

'How do you spell absolutely?'

'As you like. Now address an envelope and I will relieve you of my unwelcome presence.'

He gave the letter to the agent who was waiting to take it across the lake. Ashenden brought her the reply the same

69

evening. She snatched it from his hands and for a moment pressed it to her heart. When she read it she uttered a little cry of relief.

'He won't come.'

The letter, in the Indian's flowery, stilted English, expressed his bitter disappointment. He told her how intensely he had looked forward to seeing her and implored her to do everything in the world to smooth the difficulties that prevented her from crossing the frontier. He said that it was impossible for him to come, impossible, there was a price on his head, and it would be madness for him to think of risking it. He attempted to be jocular, she did not want her little fat lover to be shot, did she?

'He won't come,' she repeated, 'he won't come.'

'You must write and tell him that there is no risk. You must say that if there were you would not dream of asking him. You must say that if he loves you he will not hesitate.'

'I won't. I won't.'

'Don't be a fool. You can't help yourself.'

She burst into a sudden flood of tears. She flung herself on the floor and seizing Ashenden's knees implored him to have mercy on her.

'I will do anything in the world for you if you will let me go.'

'Don't be absurd,' said Ashenden. 'Do you think I want to become your lover? Come, come, you must be serious. You know the alternative.'

She raised herself to her feet and changing on a sudden to fury flung at Ashenden one foul name after another.

'I like you much better like that,' he said. 'Now will you write or shall I send for the police?'

'He will not come. It is useless.'

'It is very much to your interest to make him come.'

'What do you mean by that? Do you mean that if I do everything in my power and fail, that . . .'

She looked at Ashenden with wild eyes.

'Yes, it means either you or him.'

She staggered. She put her hand to her heart. Then without a word she reached for pen and paper. But the letter was not to Ashenden's liking and he made her write it again. When she had finished she flung herself on the bed and burst once more into passionate weeping. Her grief was real, but there was something theatrical in the expression of it that prevented it from being peculiarly moving to Ashenden. He felt his relation to her as impersonal as a doctor's in the presence of a pain that he cannot alleviate. He saw now why R. had given him this peculiar task; it needed a cool head and an emotion well under control.

He did not see her next day. The answer to the letter was not delivered to him till after dinner, when it was brought to Ashenden's little house by Felix.

'Well, what news have you?'

'Our friend is getting desperate,' smiled the Frenchman. 'This afternoon she walked up to the station just as a train was about to start for Lyons. She was looking up and down uncertainly so I went to her and asked if there was anything I could do. I introduced myself as an agent of the Sureté. If looks could kill I should not be standing here now.'

'Sit down, *mon ami*,' said Ashenden.

'*Merci*. She walked away, she evidently thought it was no use to try to get on the train, but I have something more interesting to tell you. She has offered a boatman on the lake a thousand francs to take her across to Lausanne.'

'What did he say to her?'

'He said he couldn't risk it.'

71

'Yes?'

The little agent gave his shoulders a slight shrug and smiled.

'She's asked him to meet her on the road that leads to Evian at ten o'clock to-night so that they can talk of it again, and she's given him to understand that she will not repulse too fiercely the advances of a lover. I have told him to do what he likes so long as he comes and tells me everything that is of importance.'

'Are you sure you can trust him?' asked Ashenden.

'Oh, quite. He knows nothing, of course, but that she is under surveillance. You need have no fear about him. He is a good boy. I have known him all his life.'

Ashenden read Chandra's letter. It was eager and passionate. It throbbed strangely with the painful yearning of his heart. Love? Yes, if Ashenden knew anything of it there was the real thing. He told her how he spent the long hours walking by the lakeside and looking towards the coast of France. How near they were and yet so desperately parted! He repeated again and again that he could not come, and begged her not to ask him, he would do everything in the world for her, but that he dared not do, and yet if she insisted how could he resist her? He besought her to have mercy on him. And then he broke into a long wail at the thought that he must go away without seeing her, he asked her if there were not some means by which she could slip over, he swore that if he could ever hold her in his arms again he would never let her go. Even the forced and elaborate language in which it was written could not dim the hot fire that burned the pages; it was the letter of a madman.

'When will you hear the result of her interview with the boatman?' asked Ashenden.

'I have arranged to meet him at the landing-stage between eleven and twelve.'

Ashenden looked at his watch.

'I will come with you.'

They walked down the hill and reaching the quay for shelter from the cold wind stood in the lea of the Customs-house. At last they saw a man approaching and Felix stepped out of the shadow that hid them.

'Antoine.'

'*Monsieur Félix?* I have a letter for you; I promised to take it to Lausanne by the first boat to-morrow.'

Ashenden gave the man a brief glance, but did not ask what had passed between him and Giulia Lazzari. He took the letter and by the light of Felix's electric torch read it. It was in faulty German.

'*On no account come. Pay no attention to my letters. Danger. I love you. Sweetheart. Don't come.*'

He put it in his pocket, gave the boatman fifty francs, and went home to bed. But the next day when he went to see Giulia Lazzari he found her door locked. He knocked for some time, there was no answer. He called her.

'Madame Lazzari, you must open the door. I want to speak to you.'

'I am in bed. I am ill and can see no one.'

'I am sorry, but you must open the door. If you are ill I will send for a doctor.'

'No, go away. I will see no one.'

'If you do not open the door I shall send for a locksmith and have it broken open.'

There was a silence and then he heard the key turned in the lock. He went in. She was in a dressing-gown and her hair was dishevelled. She had evidently just got out of bed.

'I am at the end of my strength. I can do nothing more.

73

You have only to look at me to see that I am ill. I have been sick all night.'

'I shall not keep you long. Would you like to see a doctor?'

'What good can a doctor do me?'

He took out of his pocket the letter she had given the boatman and handed it to her.

'What is the meaning of this?' he asked.

She gave a gasp at the sight of it and her sallow face went green.

'You gave me your word that you would neither attempt to escape nor write a letter without my knowledge.'

'Did you think I would keep my word?' she cried, her voice ringing with scorn.

'No. To tell you the truth it was not entirely for your convenience that you were placed in a comfortable hotel rather than in the local gaol, but I think I should tell you that though you have your freedom to go in and out as you like you have no more chance of getting away from Thonon than if you were chained by the leg in a prison cell. It is silly to waste your time writing letters that will never be delivered.'

'*Cochon.*'

She flung the opprobrious word at him with all the violence that was in her.

'But you must sit down and write a letter that *will* be delivered.'

'Never. I will do nothing more. I will not write another word.'

'You came here on the understanding that you would do certain things.'

'I will not do them. It is finished.'

'You had better reflect a little.'

'Reflect! I have reflected. You can do what you like; I don't care.'

'Very well, I will give you five minutes to change your mind.'
Ashenden took out his watch and looked at it. He sat down
on the edge of the unmade bed.

'Oh, it has got on my nerves, this hotel. Why did you not
put me in the prison? Why, why? Everywhere I went I felt
that spies were on my heels. It is infamous what you are
making me do. Infamous! What is my crime? I ask you, what
have I done? Am I not a woman? It is infamous what you are
asking me to do. Infamous.'

She spoke in a high shrill voice. She went on and on. At
last the five minutes were up. Ashenden had not said a word.
He rose.

'Yes, go, go,' she shrieked at him.

She flung foul names at him.

'I shall come back,' said Ashenden.

He took the key out of the door as he went out of the room
and locked it behind him. Going downstairs he hurriedly
scribbled a note, called the boots and dispatched him with it
to the police-station. Then he went up again. Giulia Lazzari
had thrown herself on her bed and turned her face to the wall.
Her body was shaken with hysterical sobs. She gave no sign
that she heard him come in. Ashenden sat down on the chair
in front of the dressing-table and looked idly at the odds and
ends that littered it. The toilet things were cheap and tawdry
and none too clean. There were little shabby pots of rouge and
cold-cream and little bottles of black for the eyebrows and
eyelashes. The hairpins were horrid and greasy. The room was
untidy and the air was heavy with the smell of cheap scent.
Ashenden thought of the hundreds of rooms she must have
occupied in third-rate hotels in the course of her wandering
life from provincial town to provincial town in one country
after another. He wondered what had been her origins. She

was a coarse and vulgar woman, but what had she been when young? She was not the type he would have expected to adopt that career, for she seemed to have no advantages that could help her, and he asked himself whether she came of a family of entertainers (there are all over the world families in which for generations the members have become dancers or acrobats or comic singers) or whether she had fallen into the life accidentally through some lover in the business who had for a time made her his partner. And what men must she have known in all these years, the comrades of the shows she was in, the agents and managers who looked upon it as a perquisite of their position that they should enjoy her favours, the merchants or well-to-do tradesmen, the young sparks of the various towns she played in, who were attracted for the moment by the glamour of the dancer or the blatant sensuality of the woman! To her they were the paying customers and she accepted them indifferently as the recognized and admitted supplement to her miserable salary, but to them perhaps she was romance. In her bought arms they caught sight for a moment of the brilliant world of the capitals, and ever so distantly and however shoddily of the adventure and the glamour of a more spacious life.

There was a sudden knock at the door and Ashenden immediately cried out:

'*Entrez.*'

Giulia Lazzari sprang up in bed to a sitting posture.

'Who is it?' she called.

She gave a gasp as she saw the two detectives who had brought her from Boulogne and handed her over to Ashenden at Thonon.

'You! What do you want?' she shrieked.

'*Allons, levez vous,*' said one of them, and his voice had a sharp abruptness that suggested that he would put up with no nonsense.

'I'm afraid you must get up, Madame Lazzari,' said Ashenden. 'I am delivering you once more to the care of these gentlemen.'

'How can I get up! I'm ill, I tell you. I cannot stand. Do you want to kill me?'

'If you won't dress yourself, we shall have to dress you, and I'm afraid we shouldn't do it very cleverly. Come, come, it's no good making a scene.'

'Where are you going to take me?'

'They're going to take you back to England.'

One of the detectives took hold of her arm.

'Don't touch me, don't come near me,' she screamed furiously.

'Let her be,' said Ashenden. 'I'm sure she'll see the necessity of making as little trouble as possible.'

'I'll dress myself.'

Ashenden watched her as she took off her dressing-gown and slipped a dress over her head. She forced her feet into shoes obviously too small for her. She arranged her hair. Every now and then she gave the detectives a hurried, sullen glance. Ashenden wondered if she would have the nerve to go through with it. R. would call him a damned fool, but he almost wished she would. She went up to the dressing-table and Ashenden stood up in order to let her sit down. She greased her face quickly and then rubbed off the grease with a dirty towel, she powdered herself and made up her eyes. But her hand shook. The three men watched her in silence. She rubbed the rouge on her cheeks and painted her mouth. Then she crammed a hat down on her head. Ashenden made a gesture to the first detective and he took a pair of handcuffs out of his pocket and advanced towards her.

77

At the sight of them she started back violently and flung her arms wide.

'*Non, non, non. Je ne veux pas.* No, not them. No. No.'

'Come, *ma fille*, don't be silly,' said the detective roughly.

As though for protection (very much to his surprise) she flung her arms round Ashenden.

'Don't let them take me, have mercy on me, I can't, I can't.'

Ashenden extricated himself as best he could.

'I can do nothing more for you.'

The detective seized her wrists and was about to affix the handcuffs when with a great cry she threw herself down on the floor.

'I will do what you wish. I will do everything.'

On a sign from Ashenden the detectives left the room. He waited for a little till she had regained a certain calm. She was lying on the floor, sobbing passionately. He raised her to her feet and made her sit down.

'What do you want me to do?' she gasped.

'I want you to write another letter to Chandra.'

'My head is in a whirl. I could not put two phrases together. You must give me time.'

But Ashenden felt that it was better to get her to write a letter while she was under the effect of her terror. He did not want to give her time to collect herself.

'I will dictate the letter to you. All you have to do is to write exactly what I tell you.'

She gave a deep sigh, but took the pen and the paper and sat down before them at the dressing-table.

'If I do this and . . . and you succeed, how do I know that I shall be allowed to go free?'

'The Colonel promised that you should. You must take my word for it that I shall carry out his instructions.'

'I *should* look a fool if I betrayed my friend and then went to prison for ten years.'

'I'll tell you your best guarantee of our good faith. Except by reason of Chandra you are not of the smallest importance to us. Why should we put ourselves to the bother and expense of keeping you in prison when you can do us no harm?'

She reflected for an instant. She was composed now. It was as though, having exhausted her emotion, she had become on a sudden a sensible and practical woman.

'Tell me what you want me to write.'

Ashenden hesitated. He thought he could put the letter more or less in the way she would naturally have put it, but he had to give it consideration. It must be neither fluent nor literary. He knew that in moments of emotion people are inclined to be melodramatic and stilted. In a book or on the stage this always rings false and the author has to make his people speak more simply and with less emphasis than in fact they do. It was a serious moment, but Ashenden felt that there were in it elements of the comic.

'I didn't know I loved a coward,' he started. 'If you loved me you couldn't hesitate when I ask you to come . . . Underline *couldn't* twice.' He went on. 'When I promise you there is no danger. If you don't love me, you are right not to come. Don't come. Go back to Berlin where you are in safety. I am sick of it. I am alone here. I have made myself ill by waiting for you and every day I have said he is coming. If you loved me you would not hesitate so much. It is quite clear to me that you do not love me. I am sick and tired of you. I have no money. This hotel is impossible. There is nothing for me to stay for. I can get an engagement in Paris. I have a friend there who has made me serious propositions. I have wasted long enough over you and look what I have got from it. It is finished. Good-bye. You will never find a woman who will love you as I have loved you. I cannot afford to refuse the proposition of my friend, so I have telegraphed to him and as soon as I shall receive his answer I go to Paris. I do not blame you because you do not love me, that is not your fault, but you must see that I should be a stupid to go on wasting my life. One is not young for ever. Good-bye, Giulia.'

When Ashenden read over the letter he was not altogether satisfied. But it was the best he could do. It had an air of verisimilitude which the words lacked because, knowing little English, she had written phonetically, the spelling was atrocious and the handwriting like a child's; she had crossed out words and written them over again. Some of the phrases he had put in French. Once or twice tears had fallen on the pages and blurred the ink.

'I leave you now,' said Ashenden. 'It may be that when next you see me I shall be able to tell you that you are free to go where you choose. Where do you want to go?'

'Spain.'

'Very well, I will have everything prepared.'

She shrugged her shoulders. He left her.

There was nothing now for Ashenden to do but wait. He sent a messenger to Lausanne in the afternoon, and next morning went down to the quay to meet the boat. There was a waiting-room next to the ticket-office and here he told the detectives to hold themselves in readiness. When a boat arrived the passengers advanced along the pier in line and their passports were examined before they were allowed to go ashore. If Chandra came and showed his passport, and it was very likely that he was travelling with a false one, issued probably by a neutral nation, he was to be asked to wait and Ashenden was to identify him. Then he would be arrested.

It was with some excitement that Ashenden watched the boat come in and the little group of people gathered at the gangway. He scanned them closely but saw no one who looked in the least like an Indian. Chandra had not come. Ashenden did not know what to do. He had played his last card. There were not more than half a dozen passengers for Thonon, and when they had been examined and gone their way he strolled along the pier.

'Well, it's no go,' he said to Felix, who had been examining the passports. 'The gentleman I expected hasn't turned up.'

'I have a letter for you.'

He handed Ashenden an envelope addressed to Madame Lazzari on which he immediately recognized the spidery handwriting of Chandra Lal. At that moment the steamer from Geneva which was going to Lausanne and the end of the lake hove in sight. It arrived at Thonon every morning twenty minutes after the steamer going in the opposite direction had left. Ashenden had an inspiration.

'Where is the man who brought it?'

'He's in the ticket-office.'

'Give him the letter and tell him to return to the person who gave it to him. He is to say that he took it to the lady and she sent it back. If the person asks him to take another letter he is to say that it is not much good as she is packing her trunk and leaving Thonon.'

He saw the letter handed over and the instructions given and then walked back to his little house in the country.

The next boat on which Chandra could possibly come arrived about five and having at that hour an important engagement with an agent working in Germany he warned Felix that he might be a few minutes late. But if Chandra came he could easily be detained; there was no great hurry since the train in which he was to be taken to Paris did not start till shortly after eight. When Ashenden had finished his business he strolled leisurely down to the lake. It was light still and from the top of the hill he saw the steamer pulling out. It was an anxious moment and instinctively he quickened his steps. Suddenly he saw someone running towards him and recognized the man who had taken the letter.

'Quick, quick,' he cried. 'He's there.'

Ashenden's heart gave a great thud against his chest.

'At last.'

He began to run too and as they ran the man, panting, told him how he had taken back the unopened letter. When he put it in the Indian's hand he turned frightfully pale ('I should never have thought an Indian could turn that colour,' he said), and turned it over and over in his hand as though he could not understand what his own letter was doing there. Tears sprang to his eyes and rolled down his cheeks. ('It was grotesque, he's fat, you know.') He said something in a language the man did not understand and then in French asked him when the boat went to Thonon. When he got on board he looked about, but did not see him, then he caught sight of him, huddled up in an ulster with his hat drawn down over his eyes, standing alone in the bows. During the crossing he kept his eyes fixed on Thonon.

'Where is he now?' asked Ashenden.

'I got off first and Monsieur Felix told me to come for you.'

'I suppose they're holding him in the waiting-room.'

Ashenden was out of breath when they reached the pier. He burst into the waiting-room. A group of men, talking at the top of their voices and gesticulating wildly, were clustered round a man lying on the ground.

'What's happened?' he cried.

'Look,' said Monsieur Felix.

Chandra Lal lay there, his eyes wide open and a thin line of foam on his lips, dead. His body was horribly contorted.

'He's killed himself. We've sent for the doctor. He was too quick for us.'

A sudden thrill of horror passed through Ashenden.

When the Indian landed Felix recognized from the description that he was the man they wanted. There were only four passengers. He was the last. Felix took an exaggerated time to examine the passports of the first three, and then took the Indian's. It was a Spanish one and it was all in order. Felix asked the regulation questions and noted them on the official sheet. Then he looked at him pleasantly and said:

'Just come into the waiting-room for a moment. There are one or two formalities to fulfil.'

'Is my passport not in order?' the Indian asked.

'Perfectly.'

Chandra hesitated, but then followed the official to the door of the waiting-room. Felix opened it and stood aside.

'*Entrez.*'

Chandra went in and the two detectives stood up. He must have suspected at once that they were police-officers and realized that he had fallen into a trap.

'Sit down,' said Felix. 'I have one or two questions to put to you.'

'It is hot in here,' he said, and in point of fact they had a little stove there that kept the place like an oven. 'I will take off my coat if you permit.'

'Certainly,' said Felix graciously.

He took off his coat, apparently with some effort, and then he turned to put it on a chair, and then before they realized what had happened they were startled to see him stagger and fall heavily to the ground. While taking off his coat Chandra had managed to swallow the contents of a bottle that was still clasped in his hand. Ashenden put his nose to it. There was a very distinct odour of almonds.

For a little while they looked at the man who lay on the floor. Felix was apologetic.

'Will they be very angry?' he asked nervously.

'I don't see that it was your fault,' said Ashenden. 'Anyhow, he can do no more harm. For my part I am just as glad he killed himself. The notion of his being executed did not make me very comfortable.'

In a few minutes the doctor arrived and pronounced life extinct.

'Prussic acid,' he said to Ashenden.

Ashenden nodded.

'I will go and see Madame Lazzari,' he said. 'If she wants to stay a day or two longer I shall let her. But if she wants to go to-night of course she can. Will you give the agents at the station instructions to let her pass?'

'I shall be at the station myself,' said Felix.

Ashenden once more climbed the hill. It was night now, a cold, bright night with an unclouded sky and the sight of the new moon, a white shining thread, made him turn three times the money in his pocket. When he entered the hotel he was seized on a sudden with distaste for its cold banality. It smelt of cabbage and boiled mutton. On the walls of the hall were coloured posters of railway companies advertising Grenoble, Carcassonne and the bathing places of Normandy. He went upstairs and after a brief knock opened the door of Giulia Lazzari's room. She was sitting in front of her dressing-table, looking at herself in the glass, just idly, despairingly, apparently doing nothing, and it was in this that she saw Ashenden as he came in. Her face changed suddenly as she caught sight of his and she sprang up so vehemently that the chair fell over.

'What is it? Why are you so white?' she cried.

She turned round and stared at him and her features were gradually twisted to a look of horror.

'*Il est pris*,' she gasped.

'*Il est mort*,' said Ashenden.

'Dead! He took the poison. He had the time for that. He's escaped you after all.'

'What do you mean? How did you know about the poison?'

'He always carried it with him. He said that the English should never take him alive.'

Ashenden reflected for an instant. She had kept that secret well. He supposed the possibility of such a thing should have occurred to him. How was he to anticipate these melodramatic devices?

'Well, now you are free. You can go wherever you like and no obstacle shall be put in your way. Here are your ticket and your passport and here is the money that was in your possession when you were arrested. Do you wish to see Chandra?'

She started.

'No, no.'

'There is no need. I thought you might care to.'

She did not weep. Ashenden supposed that she had exhausted all her emotion. She seemed apathetic.

'A telegram will be sent to-night to the Spanish frontier to instruct the authorities to put no difficulties in your way. If you will take my advice you will get out of France as soon as you can.'

She said nothing, and since Ashenden had no more to say he made ready to go.

'I am sorry that I have had to show myself so hard to you.

I am glad to think that now the worst of your troubles are over and I hope that time will assuage the grief that I know you must feel for the death of your friend.'

Ashenden gave her a little bow and turned to the door. But she stopped him.

'One little moment,' she said. 'There is one thing I should like to ask. I think you have some heart.'

'Whatever I can do for you, you may be sure I will.'

'What are they going to do with his things?'

'I don't know. Why?'

Then she said something that confounded Ashenden. It was the last thing he expected.

'He had a wrist-watch that I gave him last Christmas. It cost twelve pounds. Can I have it back?'

The First Courier

FROM 'THE THREE COURIERS'

COMPTON MACKENZIE

◆

As I mentioned in the introduction, 'The Three Couriers' has long been out of print. However, I have reason to hope that this state of affairs will soon be remedied. Meanwhile, I am glad of the opportunity to let a new generation of readers know the kind of thing they have been missing.

In a note prefacing the original edition, Sir Compton wrote: 'In order to avoid a Ruritanian air the Author has had no scruples in alluding to the Vice-Admiral commanding at Mudros. He wishes it to be clearly understood that such figures of high rank are never to be identified with actual personages. Real names will be found whenever real people are introduced.'

I understand his concern, but cannot share it. In my opinion, there was never the smallest danger of his imparting a Ruritanian air to 'The Three Couriers'.

◆

I

It was hotter than ever in that city of South-east Europe some time round about the second anniversary of the war. The bloated thermometer hanging on the shaded wall outside the main entrance of the Grand Hôtel du Monde registered 110° Fahrenheit, or rather it registered between 43° and 44° Centigrade, thus goading with a final exasperation the English and American guests who could not remember in this heat how much you multiplied and divided and added to turn Centigrade into Fahrenheit. They used to stand and argue about it on the quivering pavement outside until the smell of molten rubber or blistered leather rising from their shoes made them jump like unpricked roast chestnuts into the nearest carriage to be jogged listlessly anywhere, anywhere, it really did not seem to matter much where, in this accursed sunshine. That's what Roger Waterlow felt as he nodded in amicable dejection a good-bye to Williamson, the British Naval Attaché, with whom he had been lunching, and entered his car.

'Back to the New House, sir?' the little Cockney chauffeur asked.

Waterlow grunted a resentful affirmative. He had only surrendered to the heat a week ago and moved out of the city to get the sea air in the gimcrack summer suburb of Limani. It had not seemed worth while to move when he was expecting all the time to hear from London that a successor was on the way out to relieve him of this job ashore and enable him to take command of that Q-ship he had been promised.

'Don't call it the New House,' he said sharply.

'No, sir,' replied the little chauffeur in a mildly aggrieved tone of voice. 'But I understood you didn't care for me to call any place "home" where you're only residing temporary, sir.'

It had taken a year of driving to the various queer houses in which his chief had lodged to cure Gunton of the habit of alluding to them piously one after another as 'home'. He did not understand that the solitary feature which had made residence in them bearable for Waterlow was the consciousness of their impermanence and of their all being the very antipodes of home. Nor did he understand that to call that tawdry little villa standing alone in its withered garden on the dusty cliff at the far end of Limani the New House was to utter a most unwelcome omen. Surely, thought Waterlow, as he leaned wearily back against the burning leather upholstery of the car, surely Captain X would realize that he had outlived his usefulness ashore, and would not stand in the way of his going to sea again. There must be so many naval officers in Whitehall longing to show how well they could run an Intelligence Bureau in a neutral capital, so many naval officers whose nautical experience did not go beyond finding their way into that portion of a Channel steamer reserved for first-class passengers. The general impression in Whitehall was that life out here was a jolly comic-opera sort of affair occasionally interrupted by the despatch of long telegrams to London which gave a lot of unnecessary work to the cypherers at headquarters. But Captain X by now would have received that strong letter he had sent him ten days ago, in which surely he had been able to convince him that a new man was wanted out here. Williamson had thoroughly agreed with him at lunch that the obstruction of the Military Attaché was a bad thing for the Bureau's practical utility. It meant that all the information he sent home was being crabbed at the War Office. A new man with a few hints from himself would know how to soothe Buckworth's dignity and avoid the personal animosity which had spoilt his own relations with him. After all, it was bad policy to antagonize the soldiers. It was not much fun sending fellows into Turkey and Bulgaria to risk their lives for information which the people in London were prejudiced against beforehand. Yes, a new man out here with Crowder to help him would have much better opportunities of being useful than himself. And with all he had found out

about the movements of submarines during the past year, if
anybody had a chance to make good with a Q-ship in Aegean
waters he had that chance.

'Call it the Last House, Gunton,' he said.

The little chauffeur inclined his head gravely. He could not
take a hand from the wheel to touch his cap, for the car was
travelling too fast along the straight road out of the city between
the double rows of false-pepper trees that cast their illusory
shade upon the parched pavements. To right and left beyond
the trees stretched an undulating desert, or what seemed like
a desert, now that the summer heats had obliterated one by
one the various greens whose patchwork in the spring had
given it life. The desert was scattered sparsely with flat-
roofed dwellings which without the evidence of their cultiva-
tions looked dingy and derelict. The car thrummed on,
winding up the road inside itself like a tape, it seemed, so
straight was its course. Now, scarcely a mile ahead, the sea
showed in a glaze of silver through the gaps between the
houses that followed the sweep of Limani's dusty esplanade
round the bay. Presently, when the car slowed down to make
the turn round to the left, Waterlow was surprised by the
sight of people standing in the sun a few yards from the side
of the road. He told Gunton to stop and jumped out to see
what was the attraction that could collect a group of loiterers
at this blazing hour. Workmen had been excavating founda-
tions for a house, and it appeared that they had dug up some
remains—skeletons, half a dozen of them, which were lying
in that yellow dust, each of their skulls grinning up at the hot
blue sky through an iron collar rusted by time to a fine filigree
of metal not much heavier now than lace. Waterlow beckoned
to Gunton to come and look at them.

'Coo!' the little chauffeur gasped. 'Skelingtons!'

'They must be slaves of long ago,' Waterlow muttered to himself, half by way of information.

'Very uncomfortable place to bury anybody,' Gunton commented as he edged away from the spectacle of those remote deaths.

'Yes, that's what I've been thinking for a long time now, Gunton.'

'Enough to make anybody shiver in spite of this shocking heat,' the little man declared.

The car passed the big Limani Hotel, with its wooden pier on which people ate and drank all through the night by the very edge of the phosphorescent water, deriving from the table-cloths and napkins sodden with sea-damp an illusion of coolness. A few hundred yards beyond the hotel the road began to ascend a cliff on whose slopes villas were being erected with more speed than comeliness and furnished with more ostentation than comfort. Waterlow had agreed to move out here chiefly on Crowder's account; for his plump Number Two, notwithstanding the glory and satisfaction of his commission as an Assistant-Paymaster RNVR and the arrival from England of an outfit in which when he put it on in his own room he felt like Nelson, had begun to sag in this weather. Moreover, Waterlow had decided that when his relief arrived from London it would be kinder to spare him the intolerable heat of the capital as much as possible.

The villa that Crowder had secured for the rest of the summer was hardly two years old, which meant that it ought to be clear of bugs, and it stood in a garden surrounded by a high wall.

'Which will keep out police-spies,' Crowder had said fiercely.

'But not mosquitoes or sand-flies,' his chief had reminded him.

'That's all right, sir. You wait till you see the cage in your bedroom. I tell you, it's a treat.'

And when Waterlow had seen the wire cage which protected his bed against the mosquitoes he had agreed that the fat man had chosen their new home well.

'Marble bath,' Crowder had demonstrated importantly.

'Any water?'

The fat man had looked a little apprehensive. He had omitted to try the taps.

'Dry as the hillside from which it was quarried, you ass. I thought that would happen,' a perspiring cynic had growled.

'The pipes may only just be clogged for the moment,' the fat man had suggested with his usual air of deprecatory optimism.

'Like your brains when you took this house!'

Worse had followed. It was true that the wire cage kept out the mosquitoes and the sand-flies; but Waterlow had woken up on the first night of their occupation to feel that burning sensation on the back of the neck which is the regular prelude to a battle with massed bugs. He had switched on the electric light and watched in amazement the retreat of more bugs than he had hitherto seen in all the many other rooms he had occupied for the last eighteen months put together—bugs of every size and complexion, elderly female bugs in crinolines, elderly male bugs as dark as buck niggers, adolescent bugs with the gloss of polished maple wood, infantine bugs like incredibly active and minute rubies, a horde of these loathsome creatures of darkness scuttling away from the cleanly light.

'Bring my hammer, Crowder,' he had roared into the silence. And all through that suffocating night he had lain awake in the glare of the electric light, waiting to flatten even beyond its own abominable flatness any bug that returned to peep out from the cracks in the wooden frame to which the wire was nailed. The next day the room had been soaked with paraffin; but Waterlow had no sooner sunk into an exhausted fumy sleep than the same irritation had run like fire round the back of his neck.

'I prefer the few enterprising sand-flies that can manage to crawl through the meshes of a mosquito-net, even if they do bite me between the toes,' he had told Crowder. 'That wire frame must be broken up at once, taken out into the garden, and burnt.'

And Crowder had made one of those emotional gestures of acquiescence which a life devoted to growing liquorice in the Levant had led him to suppose was the businesslike acknowledgment of an order.

'I only hope your next commanding officer will be as charitable to your idiocy as I am,' Waterlow had said with a shake of his grizzled curly head and a smile at the back of his grey eyes.

'It's awful to think of you going, Commander W,' the Assistant-Paymaster had sighed. 'There'll be no holding these blooming royalists out here when you've gone.'

But Waterlow with the picture in his mind of that brightly painted three-masted caïque waiting for him in a secret harbour of Lemnos had not even been gratified by the teardrop shimmering in the corner of Crowder's mild and moist blue eye. Surely, surely, the news of his relief would come through from London soon. Since they had moved out to Limani he had driven in every morning himself to fetch the telegrams from the Legation. And all the way back in the car he had pored over the groups of five figures on those flimsy but

93

perhaps so weighty missives and had tried to read into 56431
—27892—47621—39654, etc., etc., such a golden sentence as
*The Vice-Admiral's application for your services has been
approved. You will proceed immediately to Mudros and report
to him on arrival. Assistant-Paymaster Crowder will take
charge until* . . . And when he had got back to the noise of the
electric fan whirring above the big polished table in the
green-shuttered work-room of the New House he had given
Crowder the telegrams from Cairo or Malta or Marseilles or
Salonica, to decode, but any from London he had decoded
himself, cursing the slowness and complicacy of the secret
service cipher. But nothing like the golden sentence so often
and so fondly imagined had yet evolved from those tangles
of five-figure groups. Instead there had been nothing but
unanswerable questions about people with impossible names
who were reported to have behaved in an improbable way in
some undecipherable place. Perhaps to-day which was the
first day he had not himself fetched the telegrams from the
Chancery, the luck would change. Perhaps at this very moment,
Waterlow thought, as he alighted from the car at the wooden
gate in the high wall round the New House, Crowder was
writing out en clair that golden sentence his heart so dearly
desired.

'Beg pardon, sir,' said Gunton with an apologetic cough.

'What is it?' Waterlow snapped impatiently, for he was
longing to hear Crowder's news.

'You did say those skelingtons was slaves, didn't you, sir?'

'Probably. That was why they had been buried in those
iron collars.'

'I see, sir. You'll excuse me for asking the question, but it
passed through my mind as I'd often said to my wife I wasn't
going to be treated like a slave. So when I saw these here slaves

I was a bit interested, me having used the word in a manner of speaking as you might say. Any orders for this afternoon, sir?'

'Six o'clock as usual.'

'Beg pardon, sir,' the little chauffeur persisted nervously. 'But would you have any objections if I went and drove my wife round to have a look at those skelingtons this afternoon? I think it might do her good.'

Waterlow laughed. The thought that this funny pinched-up little Cockney with the dyspeptic nose should be married to a splendid passionate red-haired Italian always did amuse him.

'Has Mrs Gunton been more jealous than usual lately?'

'Not more than usual, sir. But I'd jest like her to see those skelingtons for herself. Not that I'm complaining because she's a bit jealous sometimes. After all, it's very nice to know that you *can* make somebody jealous. That's what I say to myself when she gets a bit too obstropulous and starts in breaking the china. Still, I'd like for her to see what they did to slaves before things got a bit better.'

'You're becoming a philosopher, Gunton. Very well, take Mrs Gunton to look at the skeletons, and tell her the story of Socrates and his wife.'

'Do you mean that under-porter we had who pinched your pistol, or so it was said by some?'

'No; I meant your fellow-philosopher.'

The little chauffeur touched his cap, and Waterlow passed on into the house.

'What on earth . . . ?' he exclaimed when he reached the work-room and saw emerging, plump and pink as a baby from its baptismal robe, the face and bare arms of his second in command from a sheet.

'You'll really have to excuse me, Commander W,' said Crowder apologetically. 'But I must wear something, and this is the coolest thing to wear in this heat. Besides, I've been on the trot all day. I thought that blessed fish we had last night was a back-number.'

'Have you decoded the telegrams?'

'All finished,' said Crowder nervously. 'And if you'll excuse me, Commander W, I'll be back in half a jiffy.'

He did not wait for an answer, but kilted his vestment round him and hurried from the room.

Waterlow looked sharply after the fat man as he sat down before the heap of papers in his place at the big table.

He had received an impression that Crowder was beating one of those hurried retreats which were always a sign that something was wrong. He turned over the telegrams from the various centres of Intelligence. A question from Malta about a discrepancy in the spelling of a suspect's name. They wanted to be sure for the reputation of their revised black list whether he had two 'p's' and one 'd' or two 'd's' and one 'p'. Waterlow dipped his pen into the red ink which he reserved for his own use. *Say that the man's dead*, he wrote. A question from Cairo: *We are revising our black list and should like to hear if you have any further information to give us about the movements of Edward or Edmund or Edwin Dear, who was reported to be acting suspiciously in Samos on January 10, 1915. May we ask for an immediate answer?* Cairo was always so polite, and more polite than ever now when it was evidently a neck-and-neck race with Malta who should be first out with a revised black list. Waterlow wrote in his red ink: *Edward Dear does not exist. Clerk of French Vice-Consul at Vathy overheard girl address Theodore Ascarides as Teddie dear. T.D. reported as German agent under name of Teddie*

96

Dear. Nothing further discovered against him. Theodore Ascarides still interpreter at Salonica with 50th A.C. Please refer to my previous reports and copies of correspondence with A.H.Q. Salonica sent you last January.

Waterlow continued to turn over the telegrams and jot down his answers, when he could do so, as he usually could, without referring to the files and card-index kept at the central bureau in the house known as Number Ten. Then he picked up the first telegram from London, and a flush deepened the tan of his cheeks as he read it: *What is known of Queenie Walters who arrived in England three weeks ago and in answer to passport control at Southampton stated she was going to stay with Mrs Waterlow, of West Lane, Galton, Hants? Her behaviour aroused suspicion but in answer to police inquiries Mrs Waterlow stated that she was your mother. Please confirm.*

Waterlow consigned to hell that branch of Military Intelligence known as M.I.5 for a set of incompetent busybodies, although in a less exasperated moment he would readily have admitted that M.I.5 was by far the least ineffective expression of military brains that the war had hitherto produced, that it was in fact a thoroughly competent affair. Then he scribbled a hasty answer:

Personal from W for X

Earnestly request you will inform M.I.5 that I am not in habit of sending suspects from here to England without previous notification. Mrs Waterlow is my mother. Queenie Walters has been of great service to our organization. Your telegram XW 354 seems to imply doubt of my competence to manage this bureau. I have already asked several times to be relieved of my job here and returned to the Navy for special employment. Beg you will make it personal matter to secure my transfer at earliest possible moment.

And as he finished scribbling out his answer, his eyes fell on the next telegram from London:

Personal from X for Waterlow

Regret impossible to replace you. Vice-Admiral has been notified that you cannot be spared. Count on you to carry on excellent work you are doing and have put in strong recommendation for your promotion.

Waterlow blinked as if he had been hit in the face. Then he struck a match and set light to that telegram on which the writing was to have shone like gold, but which, flimsy though it might seem, was as he held it over the big metal pot that was the receptacle of all his burnt wastepaper heavy as lead. There was no need to keep a copy of that telegram in the file.

So somebody else would have that three-masted caïque so brightly painted, somebody else would sail out one night from that secret harbour in Lemnos and run before the north wind past the olive-groves of Mitylene and the scarred heights of Chios and the dragon-green gorges of the Samian mountains. Somebody else would rove that many-islanded and dancing dark-blue sea. Somebody else would haunt the coast of Sicily and look up at Etna's summit hanging like a rosy plume above the deeper twilight below. Somebody else would go about from Syracuse to Matapan and beat up from Matapan to Ithaca. Somebody else would be at sea perhaps for a year and a day in that caïque getting revictualled in the deep of night and painted every other week with different gaudy hues. And somebody else, his heart thumping, would watch on some breathless pale-blue morning a submarine nosing his way suspiciously nearer and nearer until the White Ensign would be run up and the hidden gun would speak at last. Yes, somebody else was going to have that perfectly gorgeous

quarter of an hour. And Waterlow found himself thinking
with a kind of feebleness of despair that he probably did not
grasp yet how horribly disappointed he really was. He shouted
at the top of his voice for Crowder.

'Coming, sir! Coming! I'm coming right away!' And the
fat man came quaking and slithering over his sheet into the
room like a comic Druid.

'Get these replies ciphered.'

'Yes, sir.'

Crowder eyed his chief nervously. He was wondering if he
ought to say he was glad or sorry. Finally he blurted out:

'Look here, Commander W, it's not a blessed bit of good
me pretending that it wasn't a relief when that telegram came
from London to say "carry on". You're the right man in the
right place. And I tell you straight if you'd gone I couldn't
have stuck it here with anybody else. Yes, you might have been
at sea, but what I ask is, "wouldn't the whole of this blooming
organization have been at sea too?"'

'Thanks very much, Crowder; but I don't require any
butter on my wound. Oh, and by the way, give me back that
telegram I wrote about Queenie. I want to cut out all that last
bit about my transfer.'

Crowder handed him one of the telegrams.

'This isn't the one, you ass. Wait a bit, what's this? I over-
looked this one. What is this?'

1. *We are advised from a reliable source that Demetrius*
Sophiano, late attaché in Berlin, will carry an important personal
letter with official correspondence when he returns next week via
Switzerland and Italy. This is for your information. Nothing
must be done to infringe diplomatic privilege.

2. *From same source we hear that strong pressure is being*
brought to bear upon the King to declare war on the Entente

and attack Salonica force in rear to coincide with Austrian-German advance from Monastir.

Waterlow looked at Crowder.

'This sounds like an invitation to get hold of Mr Sophiano's letters,' he said.

'Right-O,' said Crowder, as if it were the easiest matter in the world to rob a diplomat of his official correspondence, as if indeed he was willing to go out immediately, dressed as he was in a sheet, and do the job himself. Waterlow tilted back in his chair, thinking.

'Type out a paraphrase of that telegram in triplicate, Crowder,' he told him. 'I want to give copies to the Naval Attaché and perhaps to the French as well.'

Yes, he thought, tilting in his chair, while Crowder with wrinkled brow and puzzled protruding tongue applied himself to the task of paraphrasing that telegram in such a way as to avoid any chance of compromising the cipher. He looked like a chubby boy at work on a school essay. Yes, he thought, perhaps dear old X had meant this news about Sophiano to be a sop for the Q-ship. He certainly implied very cautiously that an attempt was to be made on Sophiano's correspondence. It looked as if they were beginning to wake up at last at home to the situation out here. The sense of the futility of his work which had oppressed Waterlow for so many months began to leave him. Yes, dear old X had worded his telegram without any chance of having to shoulder any responsibility for failure himself, but to anybody who knew his method it was obvious that he hoped a *coup* might be made. He had only said that diplomatic privilege must not be infringed. He had not said that no action must be taken. So Tom Tiddler really was contemplating war, was he? Well, the French had been vowing for the last six months that he was. They had been sending daily warnings to Sarrail and making each particular hair of his moustache stand up on end like quills upon the fretful porcupine and making his too, too solid flesh creep with the fancy of a concentration at Larissa and an attack from the rear in force. Probably, the imminence of Roumanian intervention was getting the Germans desperate. If Tom Tiddler was ever going to be of any service to them, this was the moment to call upon him to do his damnedest.

'Come along, Crowder, haven't you typed out that paraphrase yet?'

The fat man handed it to his chief across the table with two carbon copies.

'Now listen. Ring up the Naval Attaché and say I am coming to see him at the Legation at seven o'clock. Have the Wizard warned that I want him to tell my fortune for me at ten o'clock. I'm going to lie down now and have a siesta. Nikko can wake me at half past five with a cup of coffee, and you be ready to drive down with me to Number Ten.'

When Waterlow went off to his siesta Crowder shook his head with relief. That his chief should surrender again to the need of the siesta was a token of his surrender to being here. Ever since his hopes had been roused by the offer of that Q-ship he had refused to lead the life a sane man ought to lead in a temperature of 110° Fahrenheit. He seemed to think that he should be here for such a little while longer that it did not matter what he did.

'A jolly good lay down for two hours is just what he wants, and so do all of us; I'll cipher those blessed telegrams twice as quick after a snooze.'

Presently everybody in the New House was fast asleep. Up in his bedroom Waterlow, naked under the canopy of a mosquito-net, slept. Crowder, naked under the canopy of another mosquito-net, slept. Nikko, the big Anatolian porter, with his back against the garden door, slept. Aphrodite, the squinting Smyrniote maid-of-all-work, stripped to her shift and stockings, slept on a pallet in a corner of the kitchen. Stavro, the little Levantine waif, who had been promoted to personal attendance on Waterlow from being hall-boy at Number Ten, slept in his cupboard under the stairs.

All the world was asleep in Limani that slow sun-dogged afternoon. There was no sound except the ratcheting of the cicalas in the dusty trees and the thin horn of some assiduous mosquito dancing up and down to find a gap in the net that guarded Crowder's appetizing nudity.

II

In his little room at the British Legation Commander Williamson stretched out a pair of long legs, ran his hand through a head of hair which had more straggly ends than is usual with naval officers, stroked a big beaky nose, and finally said to Waterlow:

'I'm sorry, lad, but I don't see how it can be done. My old man would kick up a fearful stink if on my suggestion one of our t.b.d.'s stopped a neutral passenger-ship, and collared a neutral diplomat carrying the official correspondence of his Legation.'

Waterlow frowned.

'I don't see where the D.I.D.* comes into this business. If the V.A. takes action on your information it becomes his pigeon.'

The Naval Attaché beamed at Waterlow as if to assure him as genially as he knew how that he was not going to be caught by such sophistry.

* Director of Intelligence Division.

'Well, if I took it on myself to ask the V.A. to arrest Mister Sophi-what's-his-name on the high seas and take his papers from him, the Government here would squeal and half the lads at the Foreign Office would be running down Whitehall to ask the lads at the Admiralty what in blazes they thought the Navy was playing at, and then the D.I.D. would get it in the neck from the First Lord and I should get it in the neck from the D.I.D. and Sir Frederic would get it in the neck from the Permanent Under Secretary and you'd jolly well get it in the neck from me, you old pirate. And you'd get it in the neck from your old man too. You see what he says? *No infringement of diplomatic privilege.*'

'Yes, but Tom Tiddler would get it in the neck if there was anything in Sophiano's bag to implicate him in . . .'

'My dear man,' Williamson interrupted, 'even if there was a personal letter from the Kaiser to T.T. himself it wouldn't necessarily implicate T.T. And I don't think any interference with royal correspondence would be at all well seen at home, whatever there was in it.'

'This *is* a Charlie Chaplin war,' Waterlow sighed.

'You've said it, lad,' the Naval Attaché agreed. 'You know when I was torpedoed in the *Incontrovertible* and waded ashore with nothing but the strap of my wrist-watch to call my own? Well, of course, I claimed for the whole of my kit. About a month ago the watch itself was picked up on the beach, and the Admiralty have just notified me that they are deducting five pounds from my next pay and where do I want the remains sent? Some accountant has been doing his bit. If that isn't the meanest action of the war I don't know what is. And so they won't let you go to sea? Bad luck. I did my best for you in a private letter.'

'I'm sure you did,' said Waterlow. 'But if there's any chance

103

of things getting lively here I shan't so much mind. I'm sorry you won't take any concerted action over this telegram.'

'I'd love to oblige you, Pirate. But it just can't be done.'

Waterlow rose to go. In the doorway he hesitated for a moment. He was wondering whether he should tell Williamson that it was in his mind to invite the French to tackle the problem of Sophiano's dispatches. Williamson was such a good fellow that the prospect of risking anything in the way of a naval operation without taking him into his confidence beforehand was genuinely distasteful. It was natural of course that he should prefer N.O.'s to soldiers. Perhaps he liked them all the better because he had made such a mess of his own naval career. But there did seem something more fundamentally decent about them. Their conservatism and bigotry were really a boyish ignorance of the world preserved by the system of never allowing them to grow up and think for themselves; it was not a narrow-headed military incapacity to imagine any world except that small one with which the average soldier came into contact.

'What do you really think about the situation out here, Williamson?' he paused in the doorway to ask.

'What an extraordinary bird you are, Pirate!' the other exclaimed. 'Why ask a question like that holding on to the handle of the door? Come back in and squattez if you want to talk about things.'

Waterlow took his seat again on the other side of the Naval Attaché's desk.

'Look here,' he began earnestly, 'are we backing Diamantis, or is our main object to keep Tom Tiddler on the throne? Do we want these people to come in on our side, or don't we? Do we care two hoots if the French take complete control out here, or don't we? Have we considered what the Italian game is, or do we still suppose that Italy doesn't count except as a mildly amusing occupation for the Austrians? Has Sir Edward Grey got a policy, or has he merely a few Winchester notions about Europe? Is the Salonica show intended to be taken seriously, or is it not?'

'The Minister showed you that aide-mémoire which was sent to Sarrail the other day, didn't he?'

'The one which reminded him that when we agreed to send troops to Salonica it was on the definite understanding that they were not to be asked to take part in any offensive? Well, if we tie Sarrail's hands as a general, how can we expect him not to play the politician? Satan always finds some mischief etc.'

'Quite. Quite. But there it is, lad, and you and I can't change things.'

'But suppose the French are right, and T.T. does intend to join the Germans?'

'He may play with the idea, but I don't believe he'd be such an ass as to do anything. Why, we should starve him out in less than three weeks.'

'I'm not so sure about that. The harvest is in, and then all the ships available for a blockade might be engaged in embarking the remains of the Salonica force.'

'The thermometer's making you feel a bit pessimistic, isn't it?'

'Still, I do think it would be worth while knowing what Tom Tiddler's plans are,' Waterlow sighed.

'My dear old ass, do you suppose for a moment that he knows what they are himself?'

'But this telegram from London does look as if they were beginning to worry about the possibility of his coming in against us.'

'Well, why don't you go and talk to the Minister about it?'
Waterlow jumped up from his chair impatiently.

'It's no good talking to him till I have something more
definite. Would you mind very much if . . .'

But Waterlow had no time to finish his question, because
at that moment Scrutton, the Legation porter, came in to say
that the French Naval Attaché was anxious to see Commander
Williamson, and immediately on his heels came the Comte De
Caux himself.

'Ah-ha! comment vous portez-vous, mon capitaine?' cried
Williamson boisterously when his colleague entered. And,
while the two naval representatives of Great Britain and
France stood shaking hands with one another, Waterlow
laughed to himself at the thought of what a complete and
glorious joke either of them considered the other. The English
of De Caux was if anything worse than Williamson's French,
but had either of them spoken the other's language perfectly
they would not have been an iota nearer to mutual compre-
hension. Williamson treated De Caux as somebody treats a
child with whom it is one's duty to play a jolly game, and De
Caux treated Williamson as somebody treats a lunatic whom
it is one's duty to humour.

The little blond Frenchman acted in the diplomatic corps
the part of a restless, intelligent, self-willed, and badly trained
fox-terrier in a private house. He would growl at and worry
the cushions of precedent; he would lift an intellectual leg
against the old-fashioned, highly polished furniture of pro-
cedure: he would chew the ankles of fussy self-important
Monsieur Lolivrel, his own Minister; he would leap up
against the shirt-fronts of all the other Ministers, even that
particularly well starched one of Sir Frederic Ovenden, and
dapple them with the marks of his muddy paws; he was liable

to dash out into the street at any moment and snap at all the passers-by; he would take home the decayed bones of information and other rubbish to deposit them at the feet of Monsieur Briand and other members of the French Government; he would vomit up on the most scrupulously brushed diplomatic carpet a quantity of undigested facts; and he would sit for hours on the steps of the French Legation barking into the air at nothing. At the same time he was a jolly little dog and an excellent ratter when there were any real rats to catch; and though he was apt to imagine burglars when there were no burglars about, he would have been the first to attack a real one at whatever cost to himself. He had arrived here a month or two after the Army of the Orient was constituted chiefly to keep General Sarrail from making mischief in France, and it was soon evident that he had the ear of important political personages at home, unlimited funds at his disposal, and a definite policy in his wallet. He installed himself with a number of subaltern officers, all naval, at the French Archaeological School; and it had been one of Waterlow's first tasks to win the confidence of this new organization so that he could always be in a position to keep his own authorities informed of the French plans. He had only once visited the headquarters of the French School, and he had sighed a little enviously when he had seen the richly equipped staff in that cool house with its garden cypress-shaded, its marble fragments, and photographs of classic scenes, and its reproachful air of belonging to a world of academic calm, an older sweeter world. To have those statues and trees and that cloistral habitation was enough to make one envious; but to have as well all the typewriters and cars and clerks and, no doubt, all the funds one wanted was almost more than the head of a starved English Intelligence bureau could stand. Still, Waterlow reminded himself, he had anyway had nine months' start and with the fruits of those nine months he had bought the goodwill of this new and wealthy organization. Not that he came much into contact with De Caux himself. His was the bark, but the bite was Monsieur Mortier, who had charge of espionage, contra-espionage, propaganda, and indeed of all the practical side of the French Naval Attaché's activities. Waterlow had met Mortier first not at the French School, but in Williamson's room on a fine winter's afternoon, and he had immediately offered to put at his disposal all the facts he had accumulated about the enemy's underground activity. That very evening his opposite number had arrived at Number Ten to take advantage of his offer, and the two men so utterly dissimilar outwardly and inwardly had become friends. Mortier might have stood for the complete Frenchman as he really is, just as De Caux was the Frenchman as the Englishman sees him. In appearance he was small and insignificant with one of those pallid skins which to the Anglo-Saxon are the proof of grubbi-ness. A little dark scrubby moustache, a pair of lustrous long-lashed eyes, dark hair closely cut and brushed up on end, sensitive hands, always dressed in black however hot the weather, always precise in his vocabulary however much excited, and always formally polite in his gestures however bitterly insolent with his tongue, that was Monsieur Mortier. By profession he was an engineer, and in the early part of the war he had been serving in one of the big naval arsenals, from which he had been taken by De Caux and told to undermine the situation out here in the interests of his country and his political party. His own reward would be the Légion d'Hon-neur, the scarlet ribbon of which would seem to a little man so fond of dark habiliments and obscure subterranean traffick-ing a whole world of vivid colour.

'Rather a little rat, isn't he?' General Buckworth, the Military Attaché, had once observed to Waterlow; and Waterlow looking at the great stertorous creature who uttered this contemptuous criticism had suddenly realized why rats were able to be such a menace to humanity.

And now, while the two Naval Attachés were prodding one another in the ribs and laughing exaggeratedly at one another's jokes, Monsieur Mortier himself came into the room. His bright eyes smiled at Waterlow; to his chief he was coldly deferential; to Williamson he was sardonically polite. When the rib-digging was over De Caux explained that he had brought Mortier here to help him out in his bad English, adding with a bow in Waterlow's direction that had he known Monsieur Waterlow was going to be at hand he should have been more than content to rely upon his French.

Mortier came forward to say in English which, though fluent, was too much altogether for Williamson, who like most gunnery specialists was a little deaf, that owing to a *malentendu* the Vice-Admiral at Mudros had caused to be expelled from Lemnos two French *agents* occupied with the business of obtaining information from Turkey.

'Wait a minute, I haven't quite got this,' said Williamson, holding up a hand and straining puzzled ears. 'Adjuncts to what?'

'Agents, agents,' Waterlow interposed quickly. 'Mortier wants you to telegraph the v.a. that the two men he's had expelled from Lemnos are working for Captain De Caux.'

'I see,' said Williamson, grinning genially at his colleague. 'Sound lads, eh? Mais la seule chose un peu annoyant—vous me comprenez . . .'

'*Oui, oui, je comprends bien,*' De Caux snapped impatiently, for his colleague was making very heavy weather of his French.

But Williamson, smiling away with imperturbable benevolence, held on his course with his engines running at dead slow.

'La seule chose est que—que l'amiral refuse avoir—what's "any", old boy?' This to Waterlow who prompted him. 'Of course, aucun ... oui, l'amiral refuse avoir aucun agent, vous comprenez, il refuse avoir ces agents absolument. Il est très contre les agents. N'est pas que je parle le verité, Waterlow? Il refuse avoir les agents de Waterlow dans l'île de Lemnos. Alors, je suis très très misérable, mais je ne poux pas—peux pas, I mean ... vous me comprenez ... je ne peux pas vous assister. C'est beaucoup regrettable, mais mes mains ... vous comprenez ... mes mains sont absolument tied—what's tied? Oh, look here, explain that I can't do much, I'm afraid,' Williamson concluded, turning to Waterlow, who did his best to persuade an evidently incredulous and exasperated little man that the English admiral would not even allow *him* to use Lemnos as a centre for espionage.

'*Mais cet amiral est un espèce d'imbécile, mon ami*,' the French Naval Attaché spluttered. '*Mais oui, c'est idiot!* Do we makes a war or do we makes a nothing?'

Williamson beamed at his infuriated colleague and leaning across the table patted him sympathetically on the shoulder.

'Ne vous perdrez vôtre—vôtre—I mean it can't be helped. C'est beaucoup annoyant, mais nous sommes toute dans le même bateau, vous comprenez. C'est un ordre qu'il a fait.'

But De Caux would not be calmed down. He tugged at his blond moustache. He struck his head with his clenched fist; he leapt up and shook it at the ceiling; he banged it on the table; while Mortier with blazing eyes sat and bit his lips.

At last Williamson despairing of the Entente Cordiale bethought him of the telegram from London.

'Look here,' he said to Waterlow, 'ask Captain De Caux if he thinks anything can be done about this bird's correspondence? Explain that I dare not ask our old man to do anything, but say that perhaps he might ask their old man to do something about him.'

Waterlow jumped at the opportunity. Two minutes later the Allies were at peace again. De Caux with the prospect of incriminating the King forgot all about his two slighted agents, and even admitted that in this case they were no use and had never so far procured him a single useful fact about the enemy.

'*Deux crétins*,' he said.

Mortier nodded his agreement.

'If your admiral will shoot them, for me it is the same,' said De Caux generously.

'*Pour moi aussi*,' added Mortier.

'I have your permission to telegraph this information to General Sarrail?' De Caux asked.

'Anything you like, old boy, anything you like,' Williamson assured him, gazing benignly at his colleague with the expression of an uncle who has at last hit on a really successful toy for an exacting nephew.

'*Je trouve que cette dépêche est très intéressante, et même très importante*,' said De Caux to his aide, who frowned and nodded his head in vehement agreement.

'But when,' De Caux continued, looking at Waterlow, 'has this *sale type* been leaving Berlin?'

'That,' said Waterlow, 'I hope to find out very soon.'

'*C'est bien*,' murmured the dark-eyed Mortier.

The three of them had drawn close together, lowering their voices, when suddenly Williamson stood up and by his rising seemed to disperse the atmosphere of plots and stratagems as a sea-wind fog.

'Well now, bless you, my children, but I must really run along and dress for dinner,' he shouted most amiably. 'I'm dining with Christides.' This was one of the henchmen of Diamantis, the great leader of the Liberals and former head of the Government, the opponent of the King's policy of neutrality, and the passionate friend of the Entente.

'I am arriving to be very *embêté* by Monsieur Diamantis,' De Caux snarled. '*Ah, il est rasant, cet homme.* He makes nothing. He must always be waiting. *Bien sûr il faut chasser ce roi ignoble de son royaume, mais Monsieur Diamantis, ah je ne sais pas! La France* cannot be for waiting always to Monsieur Diamantis. *Mais non, c'est la barbe!*'

'Oh, I think the old gentleman knows what he's doing,' said Williamson soothingly. 'He'll move when the right moment arrives. He's a downy old bird.'

'*Hein?*'

'Je dis que il est beaucoup beaucoup sage.'

De Caux grunted. It was not a quality he much admired in anybody.

As the four of them crossed the marble hall of the Legation Williamson drew Waterlow aside:

'I wouldn't say anything to Sir Frederic about this courier business. It's a thousand to one against the Francos snaffling him, and if there's a row it's better the old man shouldn't have known anything beforehand.'

General Buckworth passed by at this moment with majestic tread. He tried not to scowl at the four nuisances, who in his opinion ought all to be afloat, or if not afloat beneath the waves, and certainly not ashore. The Military Attaché considered naval officers ashore an even more serious menace to the military situation than they were at sea.

'Poor Williamson,' he once observed to Vane-Howard in

the Chancery. 'He hardly possesses the brains of a linnet.'

And the Second Secretary who thought it as good a joke as Williamson did himself when it was repeated to him, never failed to chirrup loudly whenever he saw the Naval Attaché trying to explain some naval manoeuvre or necessity to his colleague.

'Whenever Billson tackles Buckie,' he used to chuckle, 'Buckie always looks like an old gentleman being asked the time by an errand-boy in Bond Street.'

Outside the Legation three cars were waiting in the shadow of the big pine-trees that seeming as old as Arcadia spread their mighty branches over the garden of the square.

'By gad,' Williamson shouted boisterously on the top of the steps, 'the way you sleuth-hounds make yourselves comfortable is a crying scandal. Now which of you profiteers is going to drive me back to my hotel?'

'Jump in,' Waterlow told him. Then he turned to Mortier. 'Suppose I have any news for you to-morrow night? Can you dine with me at Limani? You haven't seen my new house yet.'

'*Alors je viendrai avec plaisir.*'

'*Alors au revoir. Au revoir, mon capitaine.*'

The French Naval Attaché waved cordially to Waterlow as he mounted his car where, so full of nervous energy was he in repose, he seemed to flutter in the hot breeze like the spruce little tricolour on the bonnet, himself in that huge Panhard like the flag a miniature emblem of his country.

Waterlow beckoned Mortier to his side again.

'You won't let De Caux start babbling about his fellow Sophiano and his letters?' he murmured.

'*Ah, mon cher ami,*' said the other with a significant smile, '*le vent souffle.*'

'Yes, but try to keep him quiet. I want to find out when

Sophiano leaves Berlin before we go into any details about capturing his correspondence.'

'Come on! Come on!' shouted Williamson from the car. 'We all know you can talk French, lad. But I'm dining with old Christmas Tree at half past eight out at Ilissa.'

'*Alors à demain.*'

'*C'est entendu. Demain,*' Mortier replied, and after a ceremonious handshake with both the Englishmen he entered to Waterlow's relief the same car as De Caux. He might succeed in persuading his chief to keep his mouth shut for a day or two anyway. He knew how much tempted De Caux would be to curdle the blood of Lolivrel, the French Minister, with tales of the King's intended enormities. Then Lolivrel would go fussing round to all his colleagues and Honorati, the Italian Minister, might get alarmed that his country which was still at peace with Germany would be involved in an outrage against diplomatic immunity and . . .

'Of course, there may be nothing in it at all,' he said to Williamson as the car turned to the right of the leafy square and entered the traffic of the city's main street.

'Well, something had to be done to stop poor old Corks from tearing out any more of his hair over those two chaps Buzfuz has chucked off Lemnos. I'm awfully fond of the Francos myself, but I'd sooner try to soothe an infant with acute wind than a Franco with a grievance. I made it perfectly clear a month ago that Buzfuz wouldn't allow anybody to work spy-trips from Lemnos. Well, thanks for the lift, you old ruffian.'

The Naval Attaché jumped out of the car and ran up the steps of his hotel, glancing on his way to where with the setting of the sun the mercury in the bloated thermometer had gone down to 37°, which meant that it was now only 98°

Fahrenheit and likely not to be much more than 90° during the night.

Through that rosy violet light which every evening stained the white houses of the city for a few radiant minutes the car drove on to Waterlow's central bureau known as Number Ten. Most of the agents had gone off to their dinners; but Crowder was still there, and Henderson, who kept the card-index of the organization's activities, was hard at work as usual. He looked weary and emaciated, and the good effect of a fortnight he had recently spent on the island of Delos was no longer evident in his appearance.

'Hope you've written out a nice lurid history of Edward Dear for Cairo,' Waterlow said to him.

The scholar looked up and muttered something in his high-pitched and usually unintelligible voice. As the word was a monosyllabic plural Waterlow understood what he said and agreed.

'Not only did we send them all the details about Theodore Ascarides last February,' Henderson gabbled, 'but twice since have I sent them. Yet I suppose those military dunder-heads would call a person like myself unpractical.' Then he subsided into complete incomprehensibleness, muttering and chuckling to himself.

'What?'

'I was quoting a Greek proverb. Κάμηλος καὶ ψωριῶσα πολλῶν ὄνων ἀνατίθεται φορτία.'

'Which means?'

'Even a mangy camel can carry more than quite a lot of donkeys.'

Waterlow laughed.

'By the way, have we got anything about this fellow Demetrius Sophiano on our files?'

'No, he's *virgo intacta*,' the scholar gurgled. Then he ran a
long grubby finger along the cards, and offered the new one
he had just allotted to Sophiano with the air of a lovebird
picking out a fortune for some consultant. 'What larks if we
got his bag, guv'nor,' he gabbled. 'I'm longing to get a really
good cardful about Tom Tiddler. Real jam that would be.'

It always seemed to Waterlow when he was listening to his
chronicler that he was reading some early school story in the
Boys' Own Paper.

'You're an archaeologist even in your slang,' he once told
him.

The scholar put back the new card of Sophiano in its alphabetical niche, and Waterlow passed on into his own room. The
draperies with their pattern of the Tree of Life in blood-red
and powder-blue that muffled the walls of every room took on
in this rosy violet light a brief richness and glow of vitality,
and the grotesque cretonne landscape thronged with fabulous
beasts achieved a paradisial beauty and innocence.

'Telegrams sent off?' Waterlow asked Crowder.

The fat man put on his Jack Horner look as he proclaimed
their safe dispatch.

'And what about the Wizard?'

'He'll expect you to-night at ten o'clock,' said Crowder,
now oozing self-conscious merit.

'Anything in from the Poets this evening?' Waterlow asked.

Crowder threw back his head in a Mediterranean negative.

'Their reports are all on your desk. But there's nothing in
any of them. Too hot I suppose for them to use their brains.'

Waterlow sat down and listlessly turned over the day's
verses, protecting himself the while with a horse-hair swish
against the flies. The agent called Milton had his suspicions
of a woman and was making further inquiries. The agent

called Chaucer had his suspicions of a man and was making further inquiries. The agent called Dryden wanted three days' leave to do a job for General Arcucci, the Italian Military Attaché.

'Dryden can go,' he told Crowder. He might be wanting a *quid pro quo* presently from Arcucci.

'What are we going to do with Keats?' Crowder asked presently. 'He's been a blessed nuisance ever since they sacked him from the German Legation after the von Rangel business. His frowzy old mother came round this afternoon and tried to have hysterics in the passage. We don't want her round here, especially as I'm trying to get in touch with the new porter at the German Legation so that he'll work for us. Pipikos his name is.'

'I'm going to send Keats up to Salonica.'

'What will they say about that at A.H.Q.?'

'I'm not going to consult A.H.Q. What's the use of an agent to us who has to go about with a licence from A.H.Q. to spy on spies?'

'That's quite right,' Crowder agreed. 'But they may kick up a fuss if they find him out.'

'Find him out?' Waterlow scoffed. 'Why, they wouldn't find out Milton if I sent him up there. So you can let Keats know that I'll meet him, let me see, what's to-day, Tuesday— on Thursday evening at Maria's.'

For another hour Waterlow worked at his desk, oblivious of Crowder's appealing glances and occasional tightening of his belt.

'Well, I suppose we'd better go and get some dinner,' he said at last.

Crowder jumped up and shovelling the papers together from the table rammed them into the big safe, the door of which he shut with a clang that sounded in his ears as encouraging as a gong.

When they were seated at a table on the pavement outside the Café Apollo Crowder handed the bill of fare to his chief, and when he had told the waiter what to bring for him he gloated longingly over the big card preparatory to ordering his own dinner.

'Don't pore over that card any more. I've told you what I want,' said Waterlow.

'But I was wondering what I would eat myself.'

'I can tell you right away. You're going to have a plate of rice.'

'A what, Commander W?' the plump man asked tremulously.

'With your complaint you're not going to gorge on dainties. Order yourself a plate of plain boiled rice.'

Crowder's lips turned down in dismay like a thwarted baby's.

'But I've not eaten a blessed thing all day, Commander W,' he protested, with something like the sound of a sob in his throat.

'Rice,' Waterlow repeated firmly. 'And tell the waiter to be quick, or you won't even get that. It's already a quarter past nine, and we have to be at the Wizard's by ten.'

Perhaps if ever in the course of their association Crowder had been tempted to defy his chief he was tempted at this moment, the more so as Waterlow had ordered for himself a savoury dish of the most exquisite richness with a name in Turkish which signified that it was so delicious as to have choked the first man before whom it was set, in his anxiety to gobble it up. But he remembered that Waterlow had obtained for him a commission as Assistant-Paymaster in the

R.N.V.R. and that he owed him obedience as his superior officer.
Defiance died within him. He ordered the dish of plain boiled
rice. He even ate it when the waiter set it before him. And
when Waterlow sniffing the fragrant odours of the glorious
mess before himself observed how well they did this Turkish
dish at the Apollo he murmured a woebegone agreement,
wondering as he ate his own food if anything in the world
could taste more of nothing than plain boiled rice.

'Don't you think that I might have a little chicken as well?'
he suggested meekly.

'I wouldn't if I were you. I don't want you laid up. You're
safer on nothing but rice for two or three days.'

'Two or three days, Commander W?' Crowder quavered.

'And to-morrow morning you'd better have a dose of castor-
oil. I'll tell Nikko to bring it to you at six.'

'No, really, Commander W, please. I know it suits some
people, but it doesn't suit me. It doesn't really. A doctor told
me once I never ought to take castor-oil. It was too strong
for me, he said. He did really, Commander W. It *is* too strong
for some people.'

'Nikko will bring you up a dose at six,' Waterlow repeated
firmly. 'And now you might tell the waiter to inform the
blue-faced gentleman on our right that we are discussing
your tum-tum, not the tum-tum of the political situation out
here, and that his ears are not so scrupulously clean as to make
the sight of them flapping in my direction add anything to the
savour of my dinner.'

Crowder was thankful to have a chance of asserting himself
over somebody. So he bullied the waiter, and told him to
fetch the manager. Then he bullied the manager, who was
very apologetic and went over to the blue-faced eavesdropper
to inform him that he could not be served in a reputable

restaurant and must leave it at once. When the intruder had departed, the manager whose hair was so smooth that it looked as if it had been painted on his head, came back to express a hope that Capitaine Waterlow was satisfied with his dinner and to apologize for the behaviour of people corrupted by German gold. After this he expelled from the restaurant a blind beggar who was being led round by a diminutive child to beg alms, a man who was selling salted almonds, a refugee woman who was trying to sell a decayed rug, and a small boot-black who had taken advantage of the discussion to creep under the table and seize Crowder by the ankle with a view to cleaning his shoes. After this display of managerial authority and sympathy with the cause of the Entente he retired, twirling the waxed ends of his moustache.

'Finished your rice, Crowder?' Waterlow asked. 'Good! Then pay the bill and call a carriage. We'll see what the Wizard of Trebizond thinks about the future.'

III

Waterlow and Crowder left the carriage when they were near their destination and walked along two or three streets of a residential quarter until they came to a stretch of waste building-ground whose owner was probably waiting for his price before it went the way of so many other sites in this rapidly growing city. There was no moon; but the street lamps illuminated the wooden fence that bounded the waste ground, whose disreputable look was accentuated by the neatness and newness of the municipal pavement which had anticipated the completion of the street. Some fifty yards along a gate in this fence was reached, on which was chalked in tumbledown capitals: *ΑΠΑΓΟΡΕΥΕΤΑΙ Η ΕΙΣΟΔΟΣ*. This was not a cabalistic sign indicating the Wizard's abode; it was indeed actually nothing more than the familiar warning NO ADMITTANCE. Undeterred by the prohibition Crowder fumbled with the contraption which kept the gate from actually falling down upon its face rather than in any adequate way closing it, and managed to pull it aside for his chief to pass through. The street lamps shining over the top of the fence showed an acre of forlorn dusty ground, on which three goats were nosing about among the scattered tins and heaps of rubbish. All three of them looked up and bleated indignantly when the visitors passed by on their way toward the lamplit window of a low huddle of buildings in the far corner, as if they were anxious to point out to humanity the unsatisfactory nature of the pasturage on which they were supposed to provide the milk that must have been extracted from them with as much difficulty as blood from a stone.

'Get out of the way, you brutes,' Crowder commanded fiercely.

'Don't bully the poor creatures,' said Waterlow. 'You ought to sympathize with them now that you're on a low diet yourself.'

'I don't trust goats,' Crowder replied as a cynic might say he did not trust widows.

'But they won't touch *you*, Paymaster. Goats will eat most things I know. But I don't believe that a goat even after living on tins for several months would try to eat *you*.'

They had reached the abode of the Wizard by now, and a queer enough abode it was. A ramshackle collection of old planks, sheets of corrugated iron, bundles of reeds, squares of cardboard, and frame-lights, had with the side of a decayed tram and the roof of a newspaper kiosk been heaped up around some kind of old stable or cottage which formed a solid nucleus for the tatterdemalion additions. But if the outside was queer, the inside was queerer still. At a table in the central room, the floor of which was of beaten earth and the walls of which were of stone, sat a man as fat as one of those fat men whose bulk the curious observers of the eighteenth century liked to preserve with crude prints for the wonderment of the contemporary world in those ingenious popular magazines of the period. Not a pound less than twenty-five stone could he have weighed, and had anybody claimed another five stone for him it would have been rash to bet against even such a weight. This huge mass of flesh was studying an outspread pack of cards by the light of a paraffin-lamp. The rafters of the room were thronged with turkeys, fowls, and pigeons; and suspended immediately above his head was a stuffed crocodile without a tail. From another rafter was suspended a cradle, in which a baby was yelling at the top of its voice, not perhaps without reason, for a turkey had roosted on the foot of the cradle and was gobbling angrily at the infant. The floor was swarming with restless cats and children. The walls were papered with violently coloured pictures from the *Petit Journal*. On one shelf out of reach of the children and the cats was a row of dark blue bottles, on each of which was a label inscribed δηλητήριον, which means deleterious, or as we say, poisonous. On another shelf were bowls of goldfish, on a third cages of white and piebald mice, and on a fourth a high silk hat. Several door-ways opened into what were presumably counted as refuges among that huggermugger of building oddments which had been heaped round this central room. One caught glimpses in their interiors of more ragged children, of more goats, and occasionally of a small, dark, thin, harassed woman with a shiny yellow face like old wax, who was probably the wife of the Wizard and the mother of his numerous children. And, as if all this display of swarming life were not enough, the floor of beaten earth staged a continuous ballet of fleas, so thickly grouped in parts that one was aware of them trilling on the ankles as one is aware of sandhoppers on a beach.

This was the household of Emmanuel Pneumatikos, the Wizard of Trebizond. Some months had passed since Crowder had informed Waterlow that a refugee from Trebizond, now residing with his family in the city and earning a livelihood by telling fortunes, was anxious to put his magic services at the disposal of the British Government. He was able to cast a horoscope, to prognosticate from the cards, gaze into the crystal, read the hand, or expose the intention of fate from the lees of a coffee-cup. To these, the stock-in-trade of a sorcerer's art, he added some accomplishments of his own, such as the power to predict with equal infallibility the future by the way a cock picked up grains of corn, from the dough of cakes, from the excretions of mice, and from the entrails of goldfish. He was well versed in the law of numbers, knew how to conjure spirits, interpret dreams, counteract withcraft, reckon a woman's lovers from the spots on her finger-nails and a man's wealth from the disposition of his moles.

It transpired later that Pneumatikos had been employed by the agent called Herrick to make wax images of Crowder with whom he had quarrelled, and to stick pins into these waxen images before finally melting them over a slow fire. Either Herrick did not pay the Wizard properly for his task or else Pneumatikos himself really was, as he affirmed, struck with remorse for his conduct. Anyway, he had approached Crowder and confessed what Herrick had engaged him to do. Crowder, though of course he earnestly declared that he did not believe in such rubbish, had evidently suffered a shock, and he was most insistent that the services of Pneumatikos should be employed if possible in the interests of the Entente.

'What do you want me to hire him to do? Make a wax image of Hindenburg?' Waterlow had asked. 'Or do you propose to get on with the war by employing him to melt down some of our own generals and politicians first?'

Crowder had looked deprecatory.

'No, of course not, Commander W. No, that wasn't exactly my idea. But he says that a lot of people rather high up in society here come to consult him, and I thought that if ever you wanted to find out anything he might be able to help perhaps.'

'He won't make a wax image of me and stick pins into it if I don't employ him?' Waterlow had asked. 'He might, you know. He'd be able to melt me down a good deal quicker than you. I expect when he saw your size he jibbed at the cost of wax.'

'Ah, you joke about my fat, Commander W. But you wait till you see Pneumatikos.'

And when Waterlow had seen that vast bulk he had had to admit that jokes about Crowder's fat would cease henceforth to have as much point as formerly. Pneumatikos had fled with his family and his possessions from the Turks during the first autumn of the war and somehow or other he had managed to instal himself in that old stable in the corner of that plot of building-land. Presumably he had sent his wife and children scavenging round for the material out of which the additions to his new home had been made, and then set them to build it up, for it was impossible to imagine Pneumatikos himself doing anything but sitting at that table pondering the crystal or poring over columns of figures and horseshoes of playing-cards. Indeed to imagine him fleeing before the Turks was a little difficult, and that he should have arrived here all the way from Trebizond without losing anything more vital than the tail of his stuffed crocodile was, Waterlow decided, a definite proof of his supernatural powers.

'Ask him first what made him take up magic as a profession,' he had told Crowder.

'He says it was his name.'

'His name?'

'Yes, it means "spiritual".'

'Oh, it doesn't mean automobile tyres?'

And Crowder had laughed dutifully, though with a certain nervousness. Even if that business with the wax image was superstitious nonsense, those dark blue bottles labelled 'poison' were credible enough.

In the end Waterlow, although he might not be able to give exact information to London about the Bulgarian reserves from the way the Wizard's Minorca cock had picked up the grains of corn nor advise from the excretions of his piebald mice how far the construction of the Baghdad railway had progressed, found Emmanuel Pneumatikos a most useful intermediary. There were one or two ladies in high places, communication with whom had hitherto been difficult without arousing suspicion in this small capital where eyes and tongues were so busy and where the average inhabitant was so much more infernally observant and acute than the average Englishman or Englishwoman. The Wizard of Trebizond might prove an ideal medium for communicating with such ladies. He tested his sincerity as severely as he could before he took the risk of using him too confidentially; but since in espionage of any kind one was always ultimately at the mercy of the spy and the intermediary, whatever precautions one took, he finally decided to become superstitious and from time to time visit the Wizard for the purpose of learning what the future held in store for him. When from an unusual aggregation of black cards or from the progression of the moon over an ill-aspected planet in the eleventh house or from the peculiar pattern of the inside of a dead goldfish he was warned of treachery among his agents, he would always take care to let the warning he had received be known. And since it was seldom indeed that somebody or other in his employ was not either meditating treachery or indulging in it the Wizard's reputation as a seer was never impugned. If anything was wanting to that reputation it was supplied when the agent called Byron, who had long been suspected of trafficking with the Germans the secrets of the British organization, was at last caught coming out of the house of the notorious spy-organizer Weissmann, and after being dismissed was two days later seized with racking pains in every limb. Whether the Capitaine had used the Wizard's poisons or his enchantments, the effect on the duplex Byron had been unmistakable and the warning to the others salutary.

Yet to-night when Waterlow took his seat at the other side of the table and offered his palms for the study of those languid eyes of milky blue he did not seem to pay much attention to the words that were being puffed up from that huge heaving mass of flesh opposite. And it was not until the Wizard inquired if he had any questions he wanted to ask that he appeared to pay attention.

'Important questions,' he bade Crowder tell him, for not even to a sorcerer would Waterlow admit that he spoke or understood his language.

On hearing this the mass of flesh heaved actively, and in a moment the room was emptied of children and cats and any fowls that were not safely asleep on the rafters. They were swept out of the various doors into the dark hovels all round. The thin harassed woman with the yellow face shining like old wax was bidden to take the baby from the suspended cradle. Then the doors were shut. There was no sound except of a roosting bird shaking its feathers or of mice scrabbling in their cages, no movement except of the goldfish in the bowls and the fleas perpetually dancing on the floor of beaten earth.

In front of those languid eyes of milky blue was a crystal on an ebony stand.

'I want to ask Madame Chi if they are expecting an attaché of theirs at the Ministry of Foreign Affairs to arrive from Berlin.'

The Wizard nodded, his chins shaking.

'I want to know if he is expected to sail from Messina and when.'

The Wizard nodded, his chins shaking.

'That's all I want to know. Send the answers together with the behaviour of the moon next month to Number Ten to-morrow before eight o'clock if possible. Come along, Crowder.'

'A cup of coffee before you go?' Pneumatikos wheezed hospitably.

But Waterlow was in a hurry, and declined.

The Wizard rose painfully to escort them to the door, and as Crowder prepared to follow his chief he laid a pudding of a hand upon his shoulder.

'My salary for last month, Monsieur Crowder?' he whispered hoarsely.

Crowder dug in a hip-pocket and produced the amount in notes. The Wizard licked his thumb and counted them slowly.

'All correct?'

He nodded and signed the receipt which Crowder put before him.

'And now,' said Waterlow when he and his aide were strolling back along the empty lamplit street towards the main thorough-fare of the city, 'we'll pick up our car at the Apollo and drive back to Limani. I want to go through your accounts to-night.'

The Assistant-Paymaster groaned, not because he had been embezzling the funds of the Secret Service, but because, as usual, his chief had elected to go through the accounts just when he had decided it was about time he prepared them.

'I was going to have them ready for you to-morrow,' he suggested hopefully.

'I want to go through your accounts to-night,' Waterlow repeated.

And as they drove back to Limani Crowder assured him-self that he was the most hardly treated individual in the service of his country.

'Pity to keep yourself up late like this if you have to be woken at six o'clock with castor-oil,' said Waterlow when at half past one in the morning his harassed and ruffled aide with a sigh of relief locked his ledgers away in the safe. 'You know perfectly well that I expect the accounts to be ready on the last day of the month.'

'You don't really mean I've got to take castor-oil to-morrow morning?' Crowder quavered.

'Nikko has been given his orders.'

'But, Commander W, really . . .'

'Nikko has been given his orders,' Waterlow repeated frigidly. 'And let me add, so have you.'

'But I shan't be able to do anything all the morning.'

'You'll be able to type out your accounts, type out your list of the automobile users who have applied for benzine together

with the amounts they apply for, and then I want you to get
to work on the problem of that Turkish division which
Number 45 reported at Smyrna, but which according to the
Russian Military Attaché is in the Caucasus. You'll want to
go carefully through all our movement of troops files since the
evacuation of the Dardanelles. And now get along to bed.'

At this moment Yorghi, the big Anatolian on night-duty
came in to say that a gentleman wished to see Mr Crowder.

In a minute or two Crowder came back.

'It's Number 29,' he announced. 'He's out again already.
Says it was impossible to do anything. The Germans have
got a new man who has made his headquarters at Broussa and
who is tuning up their contra-espionage. Everybody's got the
wind up.'

'Didn't he get to Smyrna?'

'Oh yes, he got as far as Smyrna all right.'

'Well, ask him what regiments he noticed there.'

'I don't think he noticed anything. He's all of a shake still.
They nearly copped him on the way down to the beach.'

'Well, bring him in, and we'll see what we can find out
about this Turkish division.'

It was half past three o'clock before Waterlow and Crowder
got to bed, after a long examination of the stolid greasy
little agent known as Number 29 who would now go back to
his work as a barber until his nerve had sufficiently recovered
to make another attempt to reach Constantinople. But at
six o'clock Nikko brought Crowder his dose of castor-oil, and
at eleven o'clock he was sitting in his sheet groaning over that
and the statistics of benzine permits.

This was the time when one of the ragged sons of the
Wizard of Trebizond rang the bell of Monsieur Charitaki's
house and informed the parlour-maid who opened the door

that his father had sent him to tell Madame Charitaki that the lunar progressions would be ready for her at twelve o'clock. Madame Charitaki herself, a neat little woman with large bright sherry-coloured eyes, was at that moment sitting before her toilet-glass and studying with a frown a superfluous hair upon her cleft and pointed chin. When the maid came in to say that the *horoskopos* expected her at midday, Madame Charitaki started slightly, for she was consulting him more out of personal regard for Waterlow than from any desire to gratify her patriotism and devotion to the cause of Monsieur Diamantis, the great Liberal leader and friend of the Entente, who had been such a good friend to her husband and left him when he fell politically himself in secure possession of the most important desk in the Ministry of Foreign Affairs. When Madame Charitaki received from the Wizard one of these messages it was always difficult to control her heart which was apt to beat as at the sight of a love-letter. There had never been any intrigue between her and Waterlow. She had met Waterlow one night at a dance in Ilissa in the days before the bitterness between the Diamantists and the Royalists had become so sharp and when social intercourse in this factious city was still possible. They had walked about in the garden under the warm starry sky, talking politics, and out of a sudden despair for the future of her country she had begged Waterlow to let her help in any way possible to thwart the intentions of those who were leading it astray. He did not pay much attention to her enthusiasm at the time; but they met on several occasions afterwards and she was always most insistent that he should make use of her services. Finally she told him point-blank that her husband would be only too delighted to have an opportunity of being useful, and the method of communication through the Wizard was agreed upon. From that moment, of course, Waterlow was careful never to see Madame Charitaki again, and she had to make the romantic most of communicating with him through Pneumatikos. And Pneumatikos, being a fortune-teller, no doubt guessed that Madame Charitaki's love of her country was by now tangled up with her love of the English officer who paid him such a useful monthly salary, for he never failed to read in the cards that his client the Queen of Clubs was much in the thoughts of the King of Hearts. So now when Madame Charitaki's maid came in to tell her that the *horoskopos* awaited her she wasted no more time over that superfluous hair on her pointed chin, but bade her say that she would be with the wise man at noon. Madame Charitaki then set about re-dressing herself, for there was always at the back of her mind when a summons like this came the fancy that Waterlow himself might be sitting in that queer room among the cats and hens and paraphernalia of magic.

'I can tell you the answer now,' said Madame Charitaki when she sat facing the Wizard underneath his dilapidated crocodile. 'My husband was speaking this morning at break-fast of expecting Monsieur Sophiano from Berlin. He has already left Berlin and is expected to sail from Messina next week in the steamship *Byzantium*.'

The Wizard grunted with satisfaction.

'Cut twice, please,' he told her, offering the pack. He felt that she deserved an immediate reward for such a clear and decided answer to his question.

She obeyed him, fluttered and tremulous.

'Cut again with the same hand.'

He examined the horseshoe of cards.

'It is strange,' he murmured.

'What is strange?'

131

'Again this Heart man is linked with your destiny. Your husband is not a Heart man, Madame?'

'Oh no,' Madame Charitaki assured him, her sherry-coloured eyes sparkling. 'Not even Clubs. Quite definitely Spades.'

The Wizard looked at the remains of the pack in his hand, and heaved his shoulders.

'Your husband has not come out,' he wheezed.

'No,' Madame Charitaki agreed pensively. Then after buttoning her gloves she rose from the table. By the doorway she paused, bit her lip in doubt, began to say something, thought better of it, and hurried away. And as she crossed the waste ground where the goats bleated after her mournfully she insisted to herself that it would never do to give Pneumatikos any idea that she was interested in Waterlow personally. Yes, she had been wise not to suggest a meeting with him. If indeed her destiny was linked with his, why, destiny would arrange when they were to meet again. But at lunch Madame Charitaki thought that she had never heard her husband make so much noise over his food before.

Another ragged son of the Wizard's brought the answer to Waterlow's questions round to Number Ten, where he found them in an envelope on his table when he arrived after an exasperating afternoon with the movements of Turkish troops ever since the early days of Gallipoli. He sent down a man to the offices of the steamship company to find out when the *Byzantium* was expected to leave Messina, and on hearing that her departure was at least a week off, if not longer, he did not bother to go round to the French School and inform De Caux. It would be time enough to tell Mortier at dinner to-night.

Waterlow enjoyed these occasional dinners with his opposite number, and Crowder enjoyed them too, for it was his duty to plan the menu with Aphrodite, and a Frenchman, however seriously he was taking the war, could usually spare a smile for a well-planned menu. In spite of the threat of plain boiled rice Crowder had gone off cheerfully this evening a couple of hours ahead of his chief to superintend the final spasms of Aphrodite's cooking, and Crowder himself, when Waterlow and his French colleague arrived in the car together at half past eight, looked full of appetite. Nobody who had seen him vigorously shaking up the cocktail would have suspected him of being up till half past three or of being woken again at six o'clock with a dose of castor-oil. He looked as round and ruddy as the cherries he was popping with such an air into the glasses.

'Crowder has been very ill,' Waterlow said in French.

'Ah, I am sorry to hear that.'

'Oh, I'm quite all right again now,' Crowder insisted hurriedly, for the dinner was too good and companionable to be lost in exchange for a wilderness of boiled rice.

'Thanks to my prescription,' his chief added.

Stavro came in to announce that dinner was served.

'This is the wounded hero,' Waterlow told Mortier.

'Who was shot by the Boche?'

'While he was running away,' Crowder laughed.

The boy flamed up and cried out in his own language that he was not running away.

'Don't tease him,' said Waterlow sharply.

And the boy smiled his subtle cinquecento smile as like a Venetian page at some dead banquet he led the diners to the table which was laid on the terrace. Tall Nikko had put on his costume of ceremony with golden-tasselled high boots, his baggy breeches, his blue jacket piped with yellow, and waistcoat of golden moiré silk. Something like the ghost of a fresh breeze blew in from the sea. The stars were brilliant in the moonless purple sky. The crayfish was taut and succulent as it should be; the wine looked cool as amber; and for the present the mosquitoes were discouraged by the odorous smoke of the pastilles which Nikko had lighted round the terrace.

'*Ah, il fait bon ici,*' Mortier sighed.

'*Salut,*' Waterlow exclaimed raising his glass.

The little Frenchman bowed formally, and during these courtesies Crowder stuffed as much of the crayfish as he could get into his mouth before his chief remembered about the rice. But Waterlow had forgotten about Crowder's ailment, had forgotten about espionage and contre-espionage, and in the delicious languor of this hour was trying to remember the appropriate lines of Omar Khayyám.

IV

'And now, my friend,' said Monsieur Mortier when he had drained his second glass of Cordial Médoc and pushed his coffee-cup on one side, 'let us talk of our little affair.'

They rose from the table on the terrace and settled down to business in Waterlow's room. Not a word of shop had been spoken since the Frenchman had called for his host at Number Ten and they had driven off together to Crowder's entirely successful dinner. The discussion that now took place was in French.

'Sophiano has already left Berlin and will sail from Messina on the *Byzantium* next week. The exact date of sailing is not yet known here,' Waterlow announced.

Mortier frowning turned over the pages of a small note-book.

'My information is that Sophiano is already in Rome.'

'That he might easily be by now,' Waterlow interrupted.

'Ah yes, but my other information is that he will not sail from Messina with the *Byzantium* but from Naples in the *Ypsilanti*.'

It was now Waterlow who frowned.

'My source has always been a very reliable one,' he objected.

'And mine also, my friend,' Mortier insisted.

'When does the *Ypsilanti* sail for Naples?'

'A week to-day.'

'So does the *Byzantium* probably, though they said at the shipping office that she might be a day or two longer.'

'I do not think we must consider the *Byzantium*, for I can assure you that my information is perfect.'

'My dear, dear friend,' said Waterlow earnestly, 'surely you and I cannot pretend especially to one another that any information is perfect. I am willing to doubt the accuracy of mine, but I do beg you to pay our pleasant, might I say our intimate association of the last six months, the compliment of doubting your own as well.'

Mortier frowned for a moment; then with a shrug he asked Waterlow what he was expected to do.

'I don't know what your plan is yet. Tell me what you are going to do about the *Ypsilanti* and I will suggest some way of dealing with the *Byzantium*.'

'For the *Ypsilanti* it is very simple. I have in Naples a female agent who will make friends with Sophiano and speak much with him on board. So when our torpedo-boat stops the *Ypsilanti* to take from it a French woman spy they will quite naturally take her companion also. Then it will be found that her companion is a *courrier du cabinet* and we shall give to him his papers again with many apologies, but if we find

135

proposals from the Boches to attack the Army of the Orient, why, then, we shall have a very amusing stick with which to beat the King.'

'It sounds to me much too elaborate,' said Waterlow with a sigh. 'First of all, what security have you got that your female agent will make friends with Sophiano?'

'Ah, elle est *épatante*.'

'She may be *épatante* and *appétissante*, but you can't guarantee her ability to pick up Sophiano. And why do you want her in it at all?'

'That is to protect ourselves against a *gaffe*. It is impossible for us as for you to arrest a *courrier du cabinet* without a reason.'

'Well, frankly I think this variant of *cherchez la femme* the weakest I ever heard. And suppose my information is correct? Suppose Sophiano does travel in the *Byzantium* from Messina?'

'It will be easy for us to know if he travels from Messina, and in that case I have another plan which is very amusing.'

At that moment Crowder came into the room and the dark-eyed little Frenchman was abruptly silent.

'You don't mind if I tell Crowder what your original plan was?' Waterlow inquired.

'No, no,' Mortier replied sulkily, for like so many Frenchmen he always turned suspicious when in the presence of more than a single Englishman.

'The *Ypsilanti*?' Crowder said. 'But the *Ypsilanti* was sunk last month by mine or submarine—it was a question which, don't you remember?'

'I knew there was something against the *Ypsilanti*,' Waterlow laughed.

Mortier scowled.

'You are sure of that?'

'Yes, yes,' Crowder declared. And from the safe he produced the convincing account.

'I cannot understand why my informant has been so careless,' the Frenchman muttered.

'Oh, just a slip of the pen,' said Crowder gaily. He had often made such slips himself and had never been able to understand why they were always taken so seriously by his chief.

Mortier continued to scowl for a time; but his affection for Waterlow enabled him to conquer the feeling of hurt pride and presently he was finding the idea of stopping a ship that was already beneath the waves excessively *rigolo*.

'*Alors*,' he said at last. 'We must give up my plan and find another.'

Waterlow was delighted to hear it, but, as it would have been fatal to show as much, he appeared genuinely concerned, and asked why the female agent could not cast her spell on Sophiano with equal potency in Messina.

'That would not do at all,' said Mortier. 'Besides she is a very stupid creature and would certainly make a *gaffe*. No, no, it is evident that I must carry out my second plan. But what I am going to tell you now, my dear friend, is excessively confidential.'

Waterlow bowed.

'Would you rather Crowder left us together?'

'No, no,' said Mortier quickly. 'I shall be very glad if he will listen to what I am going to tell you.'

When a Frenchman makes up his mind to reveal a secret he prefers to have an audience, and in choosing Crowder as one of his confidants he was sure to obtain full value for his investment.

'I'd better lock the door, hadn't I?' Crowder suggested.

'It would perhaps be prudent,' Mortier agreed.

And then in that lucid French which lends even to the narrative of a nightmare an air of sober logic Mortier proceeded to expound the policy of his superiors.

'I must first explain that both General Sarrail and Captain De Caux are firmly convinced that the King intends to deal a *mauvais coup* if he can at the Army of the Orient. All our information is agreed upon this point. Unfortunately Monsieur Briand and other members of the Government in Paris are not yet convinced of his intentions. Monsieur Briand is much under the influence of a certain royal lady, and this makes him too ready to listen to the arguments of your Government, which of course is entirely under the influence of the Royalist idea. You will not misunderstand me, my friend, when I say that in France we find it *pénible* to be compelled at a moment when France is fighting for her existence to be hampered by an Ally with ideas of which we freed ourselves a century ago. Fortunately Monsieur Poincaré is less susceptible to the flattery of royal personages than Monsieur Briand. When Prince Theodore, the King's brother, visited Paris the other day Monsieur Briand was ridiculously polite to him, but Monsieur Poincaré was quite insulting, and told him definitely that he would listen to no complaints about the way his royal brother was treated till his royal brother could learn to behave himself in an honourable fashion toward France. Captain De Caux is quite convinced that the only policy for us to pursue is the total disarmament of the King's force and he sees no way to bring that about except a naval demonstration. His idea is to fetch the Fleet here. At present the British Government refuses to listen to this plan, and Monsieur Briand, always ready to take the side of royalty on account of the charms of a certain royal lady in Paris, makes this unwilling-

ness of the British Government his excuse not to act. Fortunately the Minister of Marine is entirely in agreement
with Captain De Caux, and there is no doubt that if we could
only convince the other members of the Cabinet of the
dangerous situation of the Army of the Orient with this traitor
of a King in our rear the action we wish to see taken would
be taken.'

'But what about Diamantis?' Waterlow asked.

'Oh, we are getting quite tired of Monsieur Diamantis.
We are always waiting for Monsieur Diamantis to make a
move, but always the reply is "Not yet. It is necessary to wait
a little longer." He seems to forget that France is fighting
for her life and that we cannot allow the Army of the Orient
to be destroyed because Monsieur Diamantis is not yet ready
to make a move. Moreover, Monsieur Diamantis is quite
ridiculous on the subject of royalty. It is really oppressive,
this idiotic preoccupation with these kings. One is suffocated
by it. And naturally when Monsieur Diamantis argues that
this country is not yet fit for a republic the British Government is only too happy to agree with him. It is quite evident
that Monsieur Diamantis will not make a revolution unless
France provides him with the necessary means. My dear
friend, you are a quite unusually intelligent Englishman, and
you will readily admit that history always teaches us the same
lesson. It is always France who must supply the men, the
money, and the ammunition for miserable little patriots to
lead their risings. *Mon dieu*, it is not difficult to make a revolution with France in the background. However, we can for the
present leave Monsieur Diamantis out of it. He sits in his
arm-chair and smiles and gives himself airs of political
wisdom; but, since he cannot trust himself to France unless
England will applaud, France must look elsewhere. The truth

is that England is *entêtée* for Roumania. Everything will go right
if only the cowardly Roumanians march, and because of this
General Sarrail has been ordered to be ready for an offensive
presently when Roumania declares war. And this is the moment
when General Sarrail is naturally anxious for his rear. It is
quite certain that the Germans will make a strong effort to
persuade the King to deal us a *mauvais coup* within the next
few weeks. The telegram which with such kindness you showed
to Captain De Caux yesterday has made a great impression
on him. He has already telegraphed to the Ministry of Marine
that the situation out here is desperate, and he has spent all
the morning in trying to persuade *ce vieux con* Lolivrel to
telegraph in the same sense to the Quai d'Orsay. Unfortunately we have here as our Minister *le plus grand imbécile*
in France, and all that Monsieur Lolivrel can say is that he
must consult his colleagues first. So this afternoon he and Sir
Frederic and the Comte Honorati and Prince Ilmenef will
meet as usual. They will talk matters over and decide that for
the moment the situation is calm. Therefore Captain De Caux
has decided that something must be done to stir up opinion in
Paris. The first suggestion was to have Monsieur Lolivrel
kidnapped and carried off to the mountains of the Epirus.'

'Kidnap the French Minister?' Waterlow gasped.

'It would be excessively amusing and it would serve him
right for being such a fool. Then we should telegraph to
the Quai d'Orsay that Monsieur Lolivrel had been carried off
by Royalist conspirators and that it is quite essential that
the Fleet must arrive here at once to protect General Sarrail.'

'You're not proposing to kidnap Sarrail too, are you?'

'No, no,' said Mortier impatiently. 'To protect General
Sarrail from the treachery of the King.'

'Yes, but I can't believe that if the King meant to declare

war on us he would begin by kidnapping the French Minister accredited to his Court.'

'But we have decided against that,' said Mortier. 'Therefore it is useless to discuss it. The only thing I regret is that such an old imbecile as Lolivrel will escape. It would have been very good for him to be carried off to the Epirus by ruffians. But we have decided on another plan. General Barraud, our Military Attaché, is to make a journey to Dyse very soon. Now he has continually contradicted every telegram that his colleague Captain De Caux has dispatched. So we have decided to blow up the line in front of his train. This will teach General Barraud that the situation out here is really desperate and perhaps his next telegram to the Ministry of War will not contradict everything that the Naval Attaché says. I am entirely disgusted with General Barraud. *Et bien*, my friend, it will be quite easy for us to arrange that General Barraud travels back from Dyse by the same train as Sophiano, and so when the explosion takes place there will be no difficulty in securing Sophiano's dispatches.'

'You're not really serious, are you?' Waterlow asked in amazement.

'Surely I am serious.'

Waterlow shook his head.

'I don't like it, Mortier. I quite agree with you that if he dared the King would attack Sarrail. But candidly I don't think that he will dare. It would give me the greatest satisfaction to secure Sophiano's letters and satisfy anyhow myself whether or not Tom Tiddler is in regular communication with the Kaiser about matters out here. But I cannot agree with you about blowing up this train. To begin with, you can't trust the fellows you'll have to employ for such a job. They'll probably bungle it and perhaps cause serious loss of life.'

The Frenchman twisted his little moustache viciously.

'It's a great pity,' he said, 'that England has not been ravaged by the Boches. You would then be better able to understand our point of view in France.'

'I'm quite at one with you over clipping the King's claws and compelling him to complete his demobilization at once if he will not come in on our side. Nobody is more anxious than I am to prove him too dangerous a character to be left at large. But why not concentrate on this courier before you start blowing up trains or kidnapping Ministers to provoke a crisis?'

Mortier frowned, and rising said coldly that he must now be going. He did not like even so much suggestion of criticism as was implied by a momentary hesitation. As a woman for an *outré* hat or dress, he demanded an immediate compliment for his most extravagant schemes; and as it is all womanhood which is wounded rather than the individual woman by a man's withholding of his admiration for some freak of fashion, so with Mortier it was national consciousness rather than his personal vanity which resented an Englishman's criticism.

'I regret very much that I have bored you with my projects,' he told his host stiffly.

'Nonsense,' Waterlow responded. 'You haven't bored me at all. I appreciate your frankness. And anyway Sophiano and his letters have become your affair, for I can't do anything about him.'

'I think we shall have him when we blow up the railway line.'

'Well, don't blow up your Military Attaché.'

Mortier tossed his head.

'I assure you, my friend, that I should not weep if General Barraud could be blown up. He is very much against Captain De Caux.'

However, the train was not blown up, because the men to whom Mortier entrusted the clockwork bombs decided that it would be more patriotic to blow up the Bulgarian Legation. So a week later they placed three bombs on the steps of the front door, wound up the bombs to explode in an hour, and retired with the money Mortier had paid them to the mountains of the Epirus. They had insisted on being paid the whole sum in advance, because, as they pointed out with irrefutable logic, should they by any chance blow themselves up as well as the railway line, their success could never be rewarded as it deserved to be. Actually, only one of the bombs did explode, and the worst damage it effected was to dislocate the front-door lock and wake the porter who had taken advantage of the departure of the staff of the Legation to a cooler residence in Ilissa to get a night's rest himself. The Entente Ministers had had to administer so many raps over the knuckles of the local authorities lately for their malevolent neutrality that it was not surprising that the local authorities should take advantage of this comic outrage to complain of the terrorism by Entente agents.

Dear Waterlow, Sir Frederic Ovenden wrote, *I am informed by the Minister of the Interior that the explosion at the Bulgarian Legation is your work. Would you be kind enough to look in and see me some time to-day or to-morrow and explain what I venture to hope is a ridiculous accusation to be made against you.*

Waterlow managed to satisfy the British Minister that neither he nor any of the men in his employment were involved in the business.

'Well, I take your word for it,' said Sir Frederic, leaning back in his worn morocco arm-chair and gazing at Waterlow over the bridge of his huge hands. 'But my impression of that tiresome little fellow De Caux is that he is trying to precipitate matters here. That's the worst of Frenchmen. There's not one of them can resist playing the Napoleoncello when he gets away from France. God knows it's difficult enough to decide how to move and what to say out here without having these diplomatic irregulars acting on their own account.'

'I think the French Intelligence is convinced the King means to spring an unpleasant surprise on us, sir.'

'French cock-a-doodle-doo!' Sir Frederic boomed contemptuously. 'It's perfectly intolerable that a silly little bantam like De Caux should be able to communicate with Paris over the head of his Minister. Not that I hold a brief for Lolivrel, who is a pompous jackass. Still, it is an intolerable state of affairs.'

Waterlow had been pondering the advantages of telling the Minister all about Mortier's exposition of the French policy. But he decided to hold his tongue. If the Quai d'Orsay chose to allow the French representatives out here to elaborate a policy of their own, and if Downing Street was incapable of discovering a policy for itself, what did it matter? What did anything matter?

'You're not looking very brilliant this afternoon,' Sir Frederic was saying from somewhere a mile away.

'Oh, I'm quite all right, sir,' he was answering in a voice that seemed to rush out of his mouth with a clatter and a roar like a train out of a tunnel.

And then Sir Frederic's six feet three inches seemed to shrink to nothing and Sir Frederic's big hooked nose went on and on, curling itself over Sir Frederic's chin and then wrapping itself round and round his neck ... round and round ... farther and farther away came Sir Frederic's voice asking him if he had his car outside. This time in trying to reply his voice stuck in the tunnel, and he could only nod . . . nod and nod and nod like a china mandarin on a mantelpiece . . . nodding and nodding and putting his tongue out.

'I hope I'm not putting my tongue out, sir?' Had he really said that?

'The sooner you get a doctor to look at your tongue the better.'

'No, no, I'm quite all right . . . perfectly all right.'

Why, they were walking down the wide marble staircase of the Legation and across the cool shady marble hall. And now Scrutton the porter had caught hold of his other arm.

'My god, this sun hits you like a cricket bat . . . very absurd to let one's teeth chatter like this . . . can't stop them some-how . . . they will rattle . . . absurd . . . doing my b–b–b–b–b–est . . . m–m–m–m–ost c–c–c–c–c–urious.'

'Is Mr Crowder out at Limani?'

'Yes, Sir Frederic.'

That was Gunton. What an absurd voice Gunton had!

'. . . and tell him to get Commander Waterlow into bed at once and to take his temperature . . .'

Queer the way the streets looked this afternoon. Parts of them were the same as usual . . . same people mincing along on the shady side . . . same shops with their blinds down on the sunny side . . . and then everybody walking about like cork-screws and the houses rolling themselves up and unrolling themselves again . . . damn this chattering . . . damned un-dignified to drive through the streets making a noise like dominoes being shuffled . . . why couldn't they build cars properly . . . impossible to lie down in a car . . . talking non-sense . . . must pull himself together . . .

'That's all right, Crowder. I shall be perfectly all right when I've lain down for a bit . . . stop this chattering in a

m-m-m-m-inute ... running into me like needles ... but
quite all right after a little rest ... Oh god, take away this
blasted mosquito-net. I don't want to lie here like a blasted
bride ... what's that about a doctor? I won't see a doctor ...
It's nothing but a Royalist plot. Who's this silly old gentleman
with a white beard? Dr Zaphiropoulos? Well, he's a suspect.
He's on our files. Tried to smuggle broad beans into Egypt
in October, 1915. Met Ananias and Zaphiropoulos in Crete
and told a lot of lies as usual. That's right, Crowder, good
man, plug my mouth up and stop my giving away any more of
our secrets ...

'Who's holding my hand?' Oh, of course it was a thermometer. 'Well, what does it say?'

'Bit of a temperature.'

That was Crowder's fat voice.

'Well, it didn't need a thermometer to tell me that. But
look here, Doctor, what I want is a long sea-voyage. Best
thing in the world for anybody. A very, very long sea-voyage.
Why don't you people settle what you're going to do and let
me get away for a long sea-voyage? Frankly, I don't mind
telling you, Doctor, that at this moment, whatever moment it
is by Eastern European time ... I don't mind telling you that
I don't feel as if I ever should be better. And between you
and me I'll go so far as to say that I don't mind a damn
whether I ever do feel better unless the weather gets cooler.
Did Crowder tell you this house was swarming with Bulgarians when we took it? Couldn't get a wink of sleep. Cunning
brutes, they used to hide under my pillow. If you're ever
troubled by Bulgarians, Doctor, get a permit from Crowder
for benzine and drown them in it.'

'The doctor's coming again later on, this evening, Commander W. Would you like a drink of barley-water?'

'Is it dark or have I gone blind now?'

'No, it's nine o'clock. You've been to sleep. I'll take your temperature again. The doctor thinks you've got a touch of sand-fly fever.'

'Crowder, I feel like death.'

'Well, you're bound to with a temperature like that.'

'How much is it?'

'Only 104° now.'

'Is that in the shade? Don't laugh in that idiotic way, Crowder. Anybody would think to hear you that I was feeling better.'

'I thought perhaps you were.'

'Well, don't think. That dreadful habit of thinking will be your ruin. It has nearly been the ruin of me. The French don't think. They act. They act the fool sometimes, but that's better than thinking and not acting at all. All my thinking won't help me to solve the problems out here. You see, the real trouble of this damned war is that most of the people at the head of affairs are just as ignorant as people like myself. And everybody is equally stupid. Otherwise of course the war would stop. You see that, don't you? All that is required to stop this war is for everybody at the head of affairs to get sand-fly fever, and then they'd see how idiotic it all is, just as I see how idiotic it all is. You think I'm delirious. I can see from your pink cornflour-mould of a face that you're convinced I am delirious. But I'm not. That's the joke of it. At this moment, whatever moment it is by Eastern European time . . . I am perhaps for the first time in my life, and certainly for the first time since I came out here, perfectly sane. The French want to send a girl to lure Sophiano to his doom. But I tried that old stock-in-trade of novelists last spring. You remember when we sent that woman all the way to Zurich to haunt, to startle, and to waylay Grigoromichelaki and steal his bag? You remember her? That great goggle-eyed lump of female flesh dusted over with Chypre, that excessively ladylike strumpet who wore shoes three sizes too small for her? Well, of course, I might have known that a man with a name like Grigoromichelaki wasn't going to be caught by that kind of pussy cat. The moment he crossed the Swiss frontier after sleeping with her he told the Italians that she was a German spy, and as soon as the Italians were perfectly sure that she wasn't a German spy they arrested her. But that's neither here nor there. The point I'm trying to make, if you have enough brains to follow me, is that there is no earthly point in collaring Sophiano. I want you to listen to me carefully now, because for all I know I shall be well in a day or two and just as idiotic as everybody else. It's perfectly clear to me at this moment that we have no right whatever to make the people here go to war with Germany. All this infernal imperialism is all wrong. And I know it's all wrong. What I object to about imperialists is that they can't even manage their own rotten creed properly. It's no use your sitting there and looking shocked, Crowder, because at the present moment, whatever the present moment is by Eastern European time, I'm delirious and therefore nothing I say can be used in evidence against me. Now Diamantis is an imperialist, but the beauty of Diamantis is that he knows what he wants. He wants an *imperium in imperio* if you know what that means, which you probably don't, because until you joined me in this tom-fool secret service show you never knew anything except how to grow liquorice. And you were then a wiser man than you are now. Diamantis wants to build up this country into a pocket empire with the help of the British Empire. That's what he calls the μεγάλη ιδέα. Now, you know the language better than me, and you know that big ideas are not always good ideas. Very well then, Tom Tiddler doesn't think this great idea of Diamantis is a good idea. Tom Tiddler would rather have a small idea. I can't explain to you now, because I'm not feeling well enough just at this Eastern European moment to explain to you all the intricacies of the personal relationship between Diamantis and Tom Tiddler. What I do want to explain is the folly of our behaviour. Do you think that I don't realize that General Sarrail wants to put Diamantis in his pocket and the whole of this city in his kit bag, and then go back to Paris and ride through the Arc de Triomphe like a circus proprietor who's made a fortune? Of course I do. But our imperialists at home, the men who have made the British Empire what it isn't, haven't the guts to see that unless we keep a tight hold of the Near East we shall lose Egypt and perhaps India. Personally I don't care a damn if we lose both. I don't care if nothing remains to us of either but Cleopatra's Needle. But that's not the point. There are a lot of wretched people in England who do care and who at this moment are firmly under the impression that their pastors and masters are taking every precaution to look after our interests out here. Well, those people think that we are backing Diamantis, and we're not doing anything of the kind. The Foreign Office, Crowder, is the Mr Micawber of the Civil Service. It does nothing but wait for something to turn up. The other day Sir Frederick telegraphed to the F.O. to ask what our policy was out here and the F.O. telegraphed back to say that we had no policy here except to exercise a mild check on the French. But if the French start blowing up trains and creating incidents how are we to stop them? Nobody seems to realize that the French intend to occupy this country. Why? Because after the war they intend to run the Near East.

So do the Italians. And so, I suppose, in our hearts do we. But what's the good of proving that Tom Tiddler is flirting with the idea of joining up with the Germans unless we are prepared to back Diamantis openly? Let Sir Frederic go to Diamantis to-morrow morning and say "Look here, go ahead, we'll support you," and I believe the old boy could raise the country. But no, that would be what Sir Edward Grey calls interfering with the domestic affairs of another country. You see we've been shouting out all over the world what Jack Horners we were over Belgium that we can't afford to admit that we've already violated the neutrality of this country. We put the blame for that on poor old Diamantis, so that the other day he had to appeal to Sir Edward Grey's honour not to say that we went to Salonica on his invitation. And though I'm working out here at what is called getting on with the war I want you to realize that while I have this fever I know that I am doing something which I hate and working for something in which I do not believe. I want to beat Germany, yes, but I want to do so by destroying submarines and not by working away here to break up a little country without any pledge that we mean honestly to build up again what we have broken. And while I am in this state, Crowder, I should like to try to get into your fat head that I am aware right inside myself that our behaviour out here is utterly inexcusable. In a day or two I shall be my unreal self again, and this nightmare of reality in which I'm wandering about at the moment, whatever the blasted moment is and wherever I am, won't mean anything. I wish I knew if the French had collared Sophiano, and I wish I knew if the Roumanians are coming in now and if the Germans and Bulgarians are going to make a big attack and if Sarrail is ready for the . . .'

Waterlow turned over and soon afterwards was asleep.

Three days later he was back at work. When he drove down to Number Ten in the car he passed the Ministry of Foreign Affairs just as a young man with glasses alighted from a carriage and walked inside with two despatch-cases. Had he waited he would have seen the young man emerge presently with one despatch-case and drive with it to the German Legation.

That evening Crowder, shining with pride, announced that he had bought the new porter at the German Legation who had taken the place of Keats and that his first item of precious information was that Monsieur Sophiano had arrived from Berlin and handed over to the German Minister several packets of letters.

I Spy

FROM 'THE BASEMENT ROOM'

GRAHAM GREENE

———◆———

Ideas of spying and being spied upon touch fantasy systems at deep and sensitive levels of the mind. Graham Greene has always seemed to find those areas of special interest; and not only in Entertainments such as 'The Ministry of Fear' and 'Our Man in Havana'. The short story upon which his screenplay, 'The Fallen Idol', was based, though not a spy story in any ordinary sense of the term, was also concerned with the knowledge of a secret, secretly acquired.

With his brother, Hugh Carleton Greene, he compiled 'The Spy's Bedside Book', a highly entertaining divertissement which appeared in 1957.

He has written only one short spy story, and here it is. It was first published in 1934.

———◆———

Charlie Stowe waited until he heard his mother snore before he got out of bed. Even then he moved with caution and tiptoed to the window. The front of the house was irregular, so that it was possible to see a light burning in his mother's room. But now all the windows were dark. A searchlight passed across the sky, lighting the banks of cloud and probing the dark deep spaces between, seeking enemy airships. The wind blew from the sea, and Charlie Stowe could hear behind his mother's snores the beating of the waves. A draught through the cracks in the window-frame stirred his nightshirt. Charlie Stowe was frightened.

But the thought of the tobacconist's shop which his father kept down a dozen wooden stairs drew him on. He was twelve years old, and already boys at the County School mocked him because he had never smoked a cigarette. The packets were piled twelve deep below, Gold Flake and Players, De Reszke, Abdulla, Woodbines, and the little shop lay under a thin haze of stale smoke which would completely disguise his crime. That it was a crime to steal some of his father's stock Charlie Stowe had no doubt, but he did not love his father; his father was unreal to him, a wraith, pale, thin, indefinite, who noticed him only spasmodically and left even punishment to his mother. For his mother he felt a passionate demonstrative love, her large boisterous presence and her noisy charity filled the world for him; from her speech he judged her the friend of everyone, from the rector's wife to the 'dear Queen', except the 'Huns', the monsters who lurked in Zeppelins in the clouds. But his father's affection and dislike were as indefinite as his movements. To-night he had said he would be in Norwich, and yet you never knew. Charlie Stowe had no sense of safety as he crept down the wooden stairs. When they creaked he clenched his fingers on the collar of his nightshirt.

At the bottom of the stairs he came out quite suddenly into the little shop. It was too dark to see his way, and he did not dare touch the switch. For half a minute he sat in despair on the bottom step with his chin cupped in his hands. Then the regular movement of the searchlight was reflected through an upper window and the boy had time to fix in memory the pile of cigarettes, the counter, and the small hole under it. The footsteps of a policeman on the pavement made him grab the first packet to his hand and dive for the hole. A light shone along the floor and a hand tried the door, then the footsteps passed on, and Charlie cowered in the darkness.

At last he got his courage back by telling himself in his adult way that if he were caught now there was nothing to be done about it, and he might as well have his smoke. He put a cigarette in his mouth and then remembered that he had no matches. For a while he dared not move. Three times the searchlight lit the shop while he muttered taunts and encouragements. 'May as well be hung for a sheep', 'Cowardy, cowardy custard', grown-up and childish exhortations oddly mixed.

But as he moved he heard footfalls in the street, the sound of several men walking rapidly. Charlie Stowe was old enough to feel surprise that anybody was about. The footsteps came nearer, stopped; a key was turned in the shop door, a voice said: 'Let him in,' and then he heard his father, 'If you wouldn't mind being quiet, gentlemen. I don't want to wake up the family.' There was a note unfamiliar to Charlie in the undecided voice. A torch flashed and the electric globe burst into blue light. The boy held his breath; he wondered whether his father would hear his heart beating, and he clutched his nightshirt tightly and prayed, 'O God, don't let me be caught.' Through a crack in the counter he could see his father where he stood, one hand held to his high stiff collar, between two men in bowler hats and belted mackintoshes. They were strangers.

'Have a cigarette,' his father said in a voice dry as a biscuit. One of the men shook his head. 'It wouldn't do, not when we are on duty. Thank you all the same.' He spoke gently, but without kindness: Charlie Stowe thought his father must be ill.

'Mind if I put a few in my pocket?' Mr Stowe asked, and when the man nodded he lifted a pile of Gold Flakes and Players from a shelf and caressed the packets with the tips of his fingers.

'Well,' he said, 'there's nothing to be done about it, and I may as well have my smokes.' For a moment Charlie Stowe feared discovery, his father stared round the shop so thoroughly; he might have been seeing it for the first time. 'It's a good little business,' he said, 'for those that like it. The wife will sell out, I suppose. Else the neighbours'll be wrecking it. Well, you want to be off. A stitch in time. I'll get my coat.'

'One of us'll come with you, if you don't mind,' said the stranger gently.

'You needn't trouble. It's on the peg here. There, I'm all ready.'

The other man said in an embarrassed way, 'Don't you want to speak to your wife?'

The thin voice was decided. 'Not me. Never do to-day what you can put off till tomorrow. She'll have her chance later, won't she?'

'Yes, yes,' one of the strangers said and he became very cheerful and encouraging. 'Don't you worry too much. While there's life . . .' and suddenly his father tried to laugh.

When the door had closed Charlie Stowe tiptoed upstairs and got into bed. He wondered why his father had left the house again so late at night and who the strangers were. Surprise and awe kept him for a little while awake. It was as if a familiar photograph had stepped from the frame to reproach him with neglect. He remembered how his father had held tight to his collar and fortified himself with proverbs, and he thought for the first time that, while his mother was boisterous and kindly, his father was very like himself, doing things in the dark which frightened him. It would have pleased him to go down to his father and tell him that he loved him, but he could hear through the window the quick steps going away. He was alone in the house with his mother, and he fell asleep.

Belgrade 1926

FROM 'THE MASK OF DIMITRIOS'

ERIC AMBLER

◆

The publisher suggested that I should include a story of my own in this collection. Regrettably, I have never written any short spy stories. 'Belgrade 1926', then, is a chapter from a novel, 'The Mask of Dimitrios'. Because of the episodic structure of the novel (it was concerned with the effort to compile a case-history of a criminal known as Dimitrios), 'Belgrade 1926' is sufficiently self-contained to read as if it might have been written as a short story. I have edited it slightly to strengthen that impression.

◆

Men have learned to distrust their imaginations. It is, therefore, strange to them when they chance to discover that a world conceived in the imagination, outside experience, does exist in fact. The afternoon which Latimer spent at the Villa Acacias, listening to Wladyslaw Grodek, he recalls as, in that sense, one of the strangest of his life. In a letter to the Greek, Marukakis, which he began that evening, while the whole thing was still fresh in his mind, he placed it on record.

Geneva.
Saturday.

My Dear Marukakis,

I remember that I promised to write to you to let you know

if I discovered anything more about Dimitrios. I wonder if you will be as surprised as I am that I have actually done so. Discovered something, I mean; for I intended to write to you in any case to thank you again for the help you gave me in Sofia.

When I left you there, I was bound, you may remember, for Belgrade. Why, then, am I writing from Geneva?

I was afraid that you would ask that question.

My dear fellow, I wish that I knew the whole answer. I know part of it. The man who employed Dimitrios in Belgrade in nineteen twenty-six, lives just outside Geneva. I can even explain how I got into touch with him. I was introduced. But just why I was introduced and just what the man who introduced us hopes to get out of it I cannot imagine. I shall, I hope, discover those things eventually. Meanwhile, let me say that if you find this mystery irritating, I find it no less so.

Did you ever believe in the existence of the 'master' spy? Until to-day I most certainly did not. Now I do. The reason for this is that I have spent the greater part of today talking to one.

He is a tall, broad-shouldered man of about sixty, with thinning grey hair still tinged with the original straw colour. He has a clear complexion, bright blue eyes and steady hands—obviously, a man with few vices who has taken good care of himself. He lives in an expensive lakeside villa with two servants and a chauffeur for the Rolls. No wife in evidence. He looks like a man quietly enjoying the well-earned fruits of a blameless and worthy career. He professes to be engaged, for recreational purposes, in writing a life of St Stephen. His nationality, I understand, was originally Polish. I may not tell you his name, so I shall call him, in the best spy-story tradition, 'G'.

G. was a 'master' spy (he has retired now, of course) in the same sense that the printer my publisher uses is a 'master' printer. He was an employer of spy labour. His work was mainly (though not entirely) administrative in character.

Now I know that a lot of nonsense is talked and written about spies and espionage, but let me try to put the question to you as G. put it to me.

He began by quoting Napoleon as saying that in war the basic element of all successful strategy was surprise.

G. is, I should say, a confirmed Napoleon-quoter. No doubt Napoleon did say that or something like it. I am quite sure he wasn't the first military leader to do so. Alexander, Caesar, Genghis Khan and Frederick of Prussia all had the same idea. In nineteen eighteen Foch thought of it, too. But to return to G.

G. says that 'the experiences of the 1914–18 conflict' showed that in a future war (that sounds so beautifully distant, doesn't it?) the mobility and striking power of modern armies and navies and the existence of air forces would render the element of surprise more important than ever; so important, in fact, that it was possible that the people who got in with a surprise attack first might win the war. It was more than ever necessary to guard against surprise, to guard against it, moreover, before the war had started.

Now, there are roughly twenty-seven independent states in Europe. Each has an army and an air force and most have some sort of navy as well. For its own security, each of those armies, air forces and navies must know what each corresponding force in each of the other twenty-six countries is doing— what its strength is, what its efficiency is, what secret preparations it is making. That means spies—armies of them.

In nineteen twenty-six, G. was employed by Italy; and

in the spring of that year he set up house in Belgrade.

Relations between Yugoslavia and Italy were strained at the time. The Italian seizure of Fiume was still as fresh in Yugoslav minds as the bombardment of Corfu; there were rumours, too (not unfounded as it was learned later in the year) that Mussolini contemplated occupying Albania.

Italy, on her side, was suspicious of Yugoslavia. Fiume was held under Yugoslav guns. A Yugoslav Albania alongside the Straits of Otranto was an unthinkable proposition. An independent Albania was tolerable only as long as it was under a predominantly Italian influence. It might be desirable to make certain of things. But the Yugoslavs might put up a fight. Reports from Italian agents in Belgrade indicated that in the event of war Yugoslavia intended to protect her seaboard by bottling herself up in the Adriatic with minefields laid just north of the Straits of Otranto.

I don't know much about these things, but apparently one does not have to lay a couple of hundred miles' worth of mines to make a two-hundred-miles-wide corridor of sea impassable. One just lays one or two small fields without letting one's enemy know just where. It is necessary, then, for them to find out the positions of those minefields.

That, then, was G.'s job in Belgrade. Italian agents found out about the minefields. G., the expert spy, was commissioned to do the real work of discovering where they were to be laid, without—a most important point this—without letting the Yugoslavs find out that he had done so. If they did find out, of course, they would promptly change the positions.

In that last part of his task G. failed. The reason for his failure was Dimitrios.

It has always seemed to me that a spy's job must be an extraordinarily difficult one. What I mean is this. If I were sent to Belgrade by the British Government with orders to get hold of the details of a secret mine-laying project for the Straits of Otranto, I should not even know where to start. Supposing I knew, as G. knew, that the details were recorded by means of markings on a navigational chart of the Straits. Very well. How many copies of the chart are kept? I would not know. Where are they kept? I would not know. I might reasonably suppose that at least one copy would be kept somewhere in the Ministry of Marine; but the Ministry of Marine is a large place. Moreover, the chart will almost certainly be under lock and key. And even if, as seems unlikely, I were able to find in which room it is kept and how to get to it, how would I set about obtaining a copy of it without letting the Yugoslavs know that I had done so?

When I tell you that within a month of his arrival in Belgrade, G. had not only found out where a copy of the chart was kept, but had also made up his mind how he was going to copy that copy *without the Yugoslavs knowing*, you will see that he is entitled to describe himself as competent.

How did he do it? What ingenious manoeuvre, what subtle trick made it possible? I shall try to break the news gently.

Posing as a German, the representative of an optical instrument-maker in Dresden, he struck up an acquaintance with a clerk in the Submarine Defence Department (which dealt with submarine nets, booms, mine-laying and mine-sweeping) of the Ministry of Marine!

Pitiful, wasn't it! The amazing thing is that he himself regards it as a very astute move. His sense of humour is quite paralysed. When I asked him if he ever read spy stories, he said that he did not, as they always seemed to him very naïve. But there is worse to come.

He struck up this acquaintance by going to the Ministry

and asking the door-keeper to direct him to the Department
of Supply, a perfectly normal request for an outsider to make.
Having got past the door-keeper, he stopped someone in a
corridor, said that he had been directed to the Submarine
Defence Department and had got lost and asked to be re-
directed. Having got to the S.D. Department, he marched in
and asked if it was the Department of Supply. They said that
it was not, and out he went. He was in there not more than a
minute, but in that time he had cast a quick eye over the
personnel of the department, or, at all events, those of them
he could see. He marked down three. That evening he waited
outside the Ministry until the first of them came out. This
man he followed home. Having found out his name and as
much as he could about him, he repeated the process on
succeeding evenings with the other two. Then he made his
choice. It fell on a man named Bulic.

Now, G.'s actual methods may have lacked subtlety; but
there was considerable subtlety in the way he employed them.
He himself is quite oblivious of any distinction here. He is
not the first successful man to misunderstand the reasons for
his own success.

G.'s first piece of subtlety lay in his choice of Bulic as a
tool.

Bulic was a disagreeable, conceited man of between forty
and fifty, older than most of his fellow clerks and disliked
by them. His wife was ten years younger than he, dissatisfied
and pretty. He suffered from catarrh. He was in the habit of
going to a café for a drink when he left the Ministry for the
day, and it was in this café that G. made his acquaintance,
by the simple process of asking him for a match, offering him
a cigar and, finally, buying him a drink.

You may imagine that a clerk in a government department

dealing with highly confidential matters would naturally tend to be suspicious of café acquaintances who tried to pump him about his work. G. was ready to deal with those suspicions long before they had entered Bulic's head.

The acquaintance ripened. G. would be in the café every evening when Bulic entered. They would carry on a desultory conversation. G., as a stranger to Belgrade, would ask Bulic's advice about this and that. He would pay for Bulic's drinks. He let Bulic condescend to him. Sometimes they would play a game of chess. Bulic would win. At other times they would play four-pack *bezique* with other frequenters of the café. Then, one evening, G. told Bulic a story.

He had been told by a mutual acquaintance, he said, that he, Bulic, held an important post in the Ministry of Marine.

For Bulic the 'mutual acquaintance' could have been one of several men with whom they played cards and exchanged opinions and who were vaguely aware that he worked in the Ministry. He frowned and opened his mouth. He was probably about to enter a mock-modest qualification of the adjective 'important'. But G. swept on. As chief salesman for a highly respectable firm of optical instrument makers, he was deputed to obtain an order due to be placed by the Ministry of Marine for binoculars. He had submitted his quotation and had hopes of securing the order but, as Bulic would know, there was nothing like a friend at court in these affairs. If, therefore, the good and influential Bulic would bring pressure to bear to see that the Dresden company secured the order, Bulic would be in pocket to the tune of twenty thousand dinar.

Consider that proposition from Bulic's point of view. Here was he, an insignificant clerk, being flattered by the representative of a great German company and promised twenty thousand dinar for doing precisely nothing. As the quotation had already been submitted, there was nothing to be done there. It would stand its chance with the other quotations. If the Dresden company secured the order he would be twenty thousand dinar in pocket without having compromised himself in any way. If they lost it *he* would lose nothing except the respect of this stupid and misinformed German.

G. admits that Bulic did make a half-hearted effort to be honest. He mumbled something about his not being sure that his influence could help. This, G. chose to treat as an attempt to increase the bribe. Bulic protested that no such thought had been in his mind. He was lost. Within five minutes he had agreed.

In the days that followed, Bulic and G. became close friends. G. ran no risk. Bulic could not know that no quotation had been submitted by the Dresden company as all quotations received by the Department of Supply were confidential until the order was placed. If he were inquisitive enough to make inquiries, he would find, as G. had found by previous reference to the *Official Gazette*, that quotations for binoculars had actually been asked for by the Department of Supply.

G. now got to work.

Bulic, remember, had to play the part assigned to him by G., the part of influential official. G., furthermore, began to make himself very amiable by entertaining Bulic and the pretty but stupid Madame Bulic at expensive restaurants and night clubs. The pair responded like thirsty plants to rain. Could Bulic be cautious when, having had the best part of a bottle of sweet champagne, he found himself involved in an argument about Italy's overwhelming naval strength and her threat to Yugoslavia's seaboard? It was unlikely. He was a little drunk. His wife was present. For the first time in his dreary life, his judgment was being treated with the deference due to it. Besides, he had his part to play. It would not do to seem to be ignorant of what was going on behind the scenes. He began to brag. He himself had seen the very plans that in operation would immobilize Italy's fleet in the Adriatic. Naturally, he had to be discreet, but ...

By the end of that evening G. knew that Bulic had access to a copy of the chart. He had also made up his mind that Bulic was going to get that copy for him.

He made his plans carefully. Then he looked round for a suitable man to carry them out. He needed a go-between. He found Dimitrios.

Just how G. came to hear of Dimitrios is not clear. I fancy that he was anxious not to compromise any of his old associates. One can conceive that his reticence might be understandable. Anyway, Dimitrios was recommended to him. I asked in what business the recommender was engaged; but G. became vague. It was so very long ago. But he remembered the verbal testimonial which accompanied the recommendation.

Dimitrios Talat was a Greek-speaking Turk with an 'effective' passport and a reputation for being 'useful' and at the same time discreet. He was also said to have had experience in 'financial work of a confidential nature'.

If one did not happen to know just what he was useful for and the nature of the financial work he had done, one might have supposed that the man under discussion was some sort of accountant. But there is, it seems, a jargon in these affairs. G. understood it and decided that Dimitrios was the man for the job in hand.

Dimitrios arrived in Belgrade five days later and presented himself at G.'s house just off the Knez Miletina.

G. remembers the occasion very well. Dimitrios, he says, was a man of medium height who might have been almost any age between thirty-five and fifty—he was actually thirty-seven. He was smartly dressed and ... But I had better quote G.'s own words:

'He was chic in an expensive way, and his hair was becoming grey at the sides of his head. He had a sleek, satisfied, confident air and something about the eyes that I recognized immediately. The man was a pimp. I can always recognize it. Do not ask me how. I have a woman's instinct for these things.'

So there you have it. Dimitrios had prospered. Had there been any more Madame Prevezas? We shall never know. At all events, G. detected the pimp in Dimitrios and was not displeased. A pimp, he reasoned, could be relied upon not to fool about with women to the detriment of the business in hand. Also Dimitrios was of pleasing address. I think that I had better quote G. again:

'He could wear his clothes gracefully. Also he looked intelligent. I was pleased by this because I did not care to employ riff-raff from the gutters. Sometimes it was necessary but I never liked it. They did not always understand my curious temperament.'

G., you see, was fussy.

Dimitrios had not wasted his time. He could now speak both German and French with reasonable accuracy. He said:

'I came as soon as I received your letter. I was busy in Bucharest but I was glad to get your letter as I had heard of you.'

G. explained carefully and with circumspection (it did not do to give too much away to a prospective employee) what he wanted done. Dimitrios listened unemotionally. When G. had finished, he asked how much he was to be paid.

'Thirty thousand dinar,' said G.

'Fifty thousand,' said Dimitrios, 'and I would prefer to have it in Swiss francs.'

They compromised on forty thousand to be paid in Swiss francs. Dimitrios smiled and shrugged his agreement.

It was the man's eyes when he smiled, says G., that first made him distrust his new employee.

I found that odd. Could it be that there was honour among scoundrels, that G., being the man he was and knowing (up to a point) the sort of man Dimitrios was, would yet need a smile to awaken distrust? Incredible. But there was no doubt that he remembered those eyes very vividly. Preveza remembered them, too, didn't she? 'Brown, anxious eyes that made you think of a doctor's eyes when he is doing something to you that hurts.' That was it, wasn't it? My theory is that it was not until Dimitrios smiled that G. realized the quality of the man whose services he had bought. 'He had the appearance of being tame but when you looked into his brown eyes you saw that he had none of the feelings that make ordinary men soft, that he was always dangerous.' Preveza again. Did G. sense the same thing? He may not have explained it to himself in that way—he is not the sort of man to set much store by feelings—but I think he may have wondered if he had made a mistake in employing Dimitrios. Their two minds were not so very dissimilar and that sort of wolf prefers to hunt alone. At all events, G. decided to keep a wary eye on Dimitrios.

Meanwhile, Bulic was finding life more pleasant than it had ever been before. He was being entertained at rich places. His wife, warmed by unfamiliar luxury, no longer looked at him with contempt and distaste in her eyes. With the money they saved on the meals provided by the stupid German she could drink her favourite cognac; and when she drank she became friendly and agreeable. In a week's time, moreover, he might become the possessor of twenty thousand dinar. There was a chance. He felt very well, he said one night, and added that cheap food was bad for his catarrh. That was the nearest he came to forgetting to play his part.

The order for the binoculars was given to a Czech firm. The *Official Gazette*, in which the fact was announced, was published at noon. At one minute past noon, G. had a copy and was on his way to an engraver on whose bench lay a half-finished copper die. By six o'clock he was waiting opposite the entrance to the Ministry. Soon after six, Bulic appeared. He had seen the *Official Gazette*. A copy was under his arm. His dejection was visible from where G. stood. G. began to follow him.

Ordinarily, Bulic would have crossed the road before many minutes had passed, to get to his café. To-night he hesitated and then walked straight on. He was not anxious to meet the man from Dresden.

G. turned down a side street and hailed a taxi. Within two minutes his taxi had made a detour and was approaching Bulic. Suddenly, he signalled to the driver to stop, bounded out on to the pavement and embraced Bulic delightedly. Before the bewildered clerk could protest, he was bundled into the taxi and G. was pouring congratulations and thanks into his ear and pressing a cheque for twenty thousand dinar into his hand.

'But I thought you'd lost the order,' mumbles Bulic at last.

G. laughs as if at a huge joke. 'Lost it!' And then he 'understands'. 'Of course! I forgot to tell you. The quotation was submitted through a Czech subsidiary of ours. Look, does this explain it?' He thrusts one of the newly printed cards into Bulic's hand. 'I don't use this card often. Most people know that these Czechs are owned by our company in Dresden.'

He brushes the matter aside. 'But we must have a drink immediately. Driver!'

That night they celebrated. His first bewilderment over, Bulic took full advantage of the situation. He became drunk. He began to brag of the potency of his influence in the Ministry until even G., who had every reason for satisfaction, was hard put to it to remain civil.

But towards the end of the evening, he drew Bulic aside. Estimates, he said, had been invited for rangefinders. Could he, Bulic, assist? Of course he could. And now Bulic became cunning. Now that the value of his co-operation had been established, he had a right to expect something on account.

G. had not anticipated this, but, secretly amused, he agreed at once. Bulic received another cheque; this time it was for ten thousand dinar. The understanding was that he should be paid a further ten thousand when the order was placed with G.'s 'employers'.

Bulic was now wealthier than ever before. He had thirty thousand dinar. Two evenings later, in the supper room of a fashionable hotel, G. introduced him to a Freiherr von Kiessling. The Freiherr von Kiessling's other name was, needless to say, Dimitrios.

'You would have thought,' says G., 'that he had been living in such places all his life. For all I know, he may have been doing so. His manner was perfect. When I introduced Bulic as an important official in the Ministry of Marine, he condescended magnificently. With Madame Bulic he was superb. He might have been greeting a princess. But I saw the way his fingers moved across the palm of her hand as he bent to kiss the back of it.'

Dimitrios had displayed himself in the supper room before G. had affected to claim acquaintance with him in order to give G. time to prepare the ground. The 'Freiherr', G. told the Bulics after he had drawn their attention to Dimitrios, was a very important man. Something of a mystery, perhaps; but a very important factor in international big business. He was enormously rich and was believed to control as many as twenty-seven companies. He might be a useful man to know.

The Bulics were enchanted to be presented to him. When the 'Freiherr' agreed to drink a glass of champagne at their table, they felt themselves honoured indeed. In their halting German they strove to make themselves agreeable. This, Bulic must have felt, was what he had been waiting for all his life: at last he was in touch with the people who counted, the real people, the people who made men and broke them, the people who might make him. Perhaps he saw himself a director of one of the 'Freiherr's' companies, with a fine house and others dependent on him, loyal servants who would respect him as a man as well as a master. When, the next morning, he went to his stool in the Ministry, there must have been joy in his heart, joy made all the sweeter by the faint misgivings, the slight prickings of conscience which could so easily be stilled. After all, G. had received his money's worth. He, Bulic, had nothing to lose. Besides, you never knew what might come of it all. Men had taken stranger paths to fortune.

The 'Freiherr' had been good enough to say that he would have supper with Herr G. and his two charming friends two evenings later.

I questioned G. about this. Would it not have been better to have struck while the iron was hot. Two days gave the Bulics time to think. 'Precisely,' was G.'s reply; 'time to think of the good things to come, to prepare themselves for the feast, to dream.' He became preternaturally solemn at the thought and then, grinning, suddenly quoted Goethe at me.

Ach! warum, ihr Götter, ist unendlich, alles, alles, endlich unser Glück nur? G., you see, lays claim to a sense of humour. That supper was the critical moment for him. Dimitrios got to work on Madame. It was such a pleasure to meet such pleasant people as Madame—and, of course, her husband. She—and her husband, naturally—must certainly come and stay with him in Bavaria next month. He preferred it to his Paris house and Cannes was sometimes chilly in the spring. Madame would enjoy Bavaria; and so, no doubt, would her husband. That was, if he could tear himself away from the Ministry.

Crude, simple stuff, no doubt; but the Bulics were crude, simple people. Madame lapped it up with her sweet champagne while Bulic became sulky. Then the great moment arrived.

The flower girl stopped by the table with her tray of orchids. Dimitrios turned round and, selecting the largest and most expensive bloom, handed it with a little flourish to Madame Bulic with a request that she accept it as a token of his esteem. Madame would accept it. Dimitrios drew out his wallet to pay. The next moment a thick wad of thousand-dinar notes fell from his breast pocket on to the table.

With a word of apology Dimitrios put the money back in his pocket. G., taking his cue, remarked that it was rather a lot of money to carry in one's pocket and asked if the 'Freiherr' always carried as much. No, he did not. He had won the money at Alessandro's earlier in the evening and had forgotten to leave it upstairs in his room. Did Madame know Alessandro's? She did not. Both the Bulics were silent as the 'Freiherr' talked on: they had never seen so much money before. In the 'Freiherr's' opinion Alessandro's was the most reliable gambling place in Belgrade. It was your own luck not the croupier's skill that mattered at Alessandro's. Personally he was having a run of luck that evening—this with velvety eyes on Madame—and had won a little more than usual. He hesitated at that point. And then: 'As you have never been in the place, I should be delighted if you would accompany me as my guests later.'

Of course, they went; and, of course, they were expected and preparations had been made. Dimitrios had arranged everything. No roulette—it is difficult to cheat a man at roulette—but there was *trente et quarante*. The minimum stake was two hundred and fifty dinar.

They had drinks and watched the play for a time. Then G. decided that he would play a little. They watched him win twice. Then the 'Freiherr' asked Madame if she would like to play. She looked at her husband. He said, apologetically, that he had very little money with him. But Dimitrios was ready for that. No trouble at all, Herr Bulic! He personally was well known to Alessandro. Any friend of his could be accommodated. If he should happen to lose a few dinar, Alessandro would take a cheque or a note.

The farce went on. Alessandro was summoned and introduced. The situation was explained to him. He raised protesting hands. Any friend of the 'Freiherr' need not even ask such a thing. Besides, he had not yet played. Time to talk of such things if he had a little bad luck.

G. thinks that if Dimitrios had allowed the two to talk to to one another for even a moment, they would not have played. Two hundred and fifty dinar was the minimum stake, and not even the possession of thirty thousand could overcome their consciousness of the value in terms of food and rent of two hundred and fifty. But Dimitrios did not give them a chance to exchange misgivings. Instead, as they were waiting at the table behind G.'s chair, he murmured to Bulic that if he, Bulic, had time, he, the 'Freiherr', would like to talk business with him over luncheon one day that week.

It was beautifully timed. It could, I feel, have meant only one thing to Bulic: 'My dear Bulic, there really is no need for you to concern yourself over a paltry few hundred dinar. I am interested in you, and that means that your fortune is made. Please do not disappoint me by showing yourself less important than you seem now.'

Madame Bulic began to play.

Her first two hundred and fifty she lost on *couleur*. The second won on *inverse*. Then, Dimitrios, advising greater caution, suggested that she play *à cheval*. There was a *refait* and then a second *refait*. Ultimately she lost again.

At the end of an hour the five thousand dinar's worth of chips she had been given had gone. Dimitrios, sympathizing with her for her 'bad luck', pushed across some five-hundred-dinar chips from a pile in front of him and begged that she would play with them 'for luck'.

The tortured Bulic may have had the idea that these were a gift, for he made only the faintest sound of protest. That they had not been a gift he was presently to discover. Madame Bulic, thoroughly miserable now and becoming a little untidy, played on. She won a little; she lost more. At half past two Bulic signed a promissory note to Alessandro for twelve thousand dinar. G. bought them a drink.

It is easy to picture the scene between the Bulics when at last they were alone—the recriminations, the tears, the interminable arguments—only too easy. Yet, bad as things were, the gloom was not unrelieved; for Bulic was to lunch the following day with the 'Freiherr'. And they were to talk business.

They did talk business. Dimitrios had been told to be encouraging. No doubt he was. Hints of big deals afoot, of opportunities for making fabulous sums for those who were in the know, talk of castles in Bavaria—it would all be there. Bulic had only to listen and let his heart beat faster. What did twelve thousand dinar matter? You had to think in millions.

All the same, it was Dimitrios who raised the subject of his guest's debt to Alessandro. He supposed that Bulic would be going along that very night to settle it. He personally would be playing again. One could not, after all, win so much without giving Alessandro a chance to lose some more. Supposing that they went along together—just the two of them. Women were bad gamblers.

When they met that night Bulic had nearly thirty-five thousand dinar in his pocket. He must have added his savings to G.'s thirty thousand. When Dimitrios reported to G.—in the early hours of the following morning—he said that Bulic had, in spite of Alessandro's protests, insisted on redeeming his promissory note before he started to play. 'I pay my debts,' he told Dimitrios proudly. The balance of the money he spent, with a flourish, on five-hundred-dinar chips. To-night he was going to make a killing. He refused a drink. He meant to keep a cool head.

G. grinned at this and perhaps he was wise to do so. Pity is sometimes too uncomfortable; and I do find Bulic pitiable. You may say that he was a weak fool. So he was. But Providence is never quite as calculating as were G. and Dimitrios. It may bludgeon away at a man, but it never feels between his ribs with a knife. Bulic had no chance. They understood him and used their understanding with devilish skill. With the cards as neatly stacked against me as they were against him, I should perhaps be no less weak, no less foolish. It is a comfort to me to believe that the occasion is unlikely to arise.

Inevitably he lost. He began to play with just over forty chips. It took him two hours of winning and losing to get rid of them. Then, quite calmly, he took another twenty on credit. He said that his luck must change. The poor wretch did not even suspect that he might be being cheated. Why should he suspect? The 'Freiherr' was losing even more than he was. He doubled his stakes and survived for forty minutes. He borrowed again and lost again. He had lost thirty-eight thousand dinar more than he had in the world when, white and sweating, he decided to stop.

After that it was plain sailing for Dimitrios. The following night Bulic returned. They let him win thirty thousand back. The third night he lost another fourteen thousand. On the fourth night, when he was about twenty-five thousand in debt, Alessandro asked for his money. Bulic promised to redeem his notes within a week. The first person to whom he went for help was G.

G. was sympathetic. Twenty-five thousand was a lot of money, wasn't it? Of course, any money he used in connection with orders received was his employers', and he was not empowered to do what he liked with it. But he himself could spare two hundred and fifty for a few days if it were any help. He would have liked to do more, but . . . Bulic took the two hundred and fifty.

With it G. gave him a word of advice. The 'Freiherr' was the man to get him out of his difficulty. He never lent money—with him it was a question of principle, he believed—but he had a reputation for helping his friends by putting them in the way of earning quite substantial sums. Why not have a talk with him?

The 'talk' between Bulic and Dimitrios took place after a dinner for which Bulic paid and in the 'Freiherr's' hotel sitting-room. G. was out of sight in the adjoining bedroom. When Bulic at last got to the point, he asked about Alessandro. Would he insist on his money? What would happen if he were not paid?

Dimitrios affected surprise. There was no question, he hoped, of Alessandro's not being paid. After all, it was on his personal recommendation that Alessandro had given credit in the first place. He would not like there to be any unpleasantness. What sort of unpleasantness? Well, Alessandro held the promissory notes and could take the matter to the police. He hoped sincerely that that would not happen.

Bulic was hoping so, too. Now, he had everything to lose, including his post at the Ministry. It might even come out that he had taken money from G. That might even mean prison. Would they believe that he had done nothing in return for those thirty thousand dinar? It was madness to expect them to do so. His only chance was to get the money from the 'Freiherr' —somehow.

To his pleas for a loan Dimitrios shook his head. No. That would simply make matters worse, for then he would owe the money to a friend instead of to an enemy; besides, it was a matter of principle with him. At the same time, he wanted to help. There was just one way; but would Herr Bulic feel disposed to take it? That was the question. He scarcely liked to mention the matter; but, since Herr Bulic pressed him, he knew of certain persons who were interested in obtaining some information from the Ministry of Marine that could not be obtained through the usual channels. They could probably be persuaded to pay as much as fifty thousand dinar for this information if they could rely upon its being accurate.

G. said that he attributed quite a lot of the success of his plan (he deems it successful in the same way that a surgeon deems an operation successful when the patient leaves the operating theatre alive) to his careful use of figures. Every sum from the original twenty thousand dinar to the amounts of the successive debts to Alessandro (who was an Italian agent) and the final amount offered by Dimitrios was carefully calculated with an eye to its psychological value. That final fifty thousand, for example. Its appeal to Bulic was two-fold. It would pay off his debt and still leave him with nearly as much as he had had before he met the 'Freiherr'. To the incentive of fear they added that of greed.

But Bulic did not give in immediately. When he heard exactly what the information was, he became frightened and angry. The anger was dealt with very efficiently by Dimitrios. If Bulic had begun to entertain doubts about the *bona fides* of the 'Freiherr' those doubts were now made certainties; for when he shouted 'dirty spy', the 'Freiherr's' easy charm deserted him. Bulic was kicked in the abdomen and then, as he bent forward retching, in the face. Gasping for breath and with pain and bleeding at the mouth, he was flung into a chair while Dimitrios explained coldly that the only risk he ran was in not doing as he was told.

His instructions were simple. Bulic was to get a copy of the chart and bring it to the hotel when he left the Ministry the following evening. An hour later the chart would be returned to him to replace in the morning. That was all. He would be paid when he brought the chart. He was warned of the consequences to himself if he should decide to go to the authorities with his story, reminded of the fifty thousand that awaited him and dismissed.

He duly returned the following night with the chart folded in four under his coat. Dimitrios took the chart in to G. and returned to keep watch on Bulic while it was photographed and the negative developed. Apparently Bulic had nothing to say. When G. had finished he took the money and the chart from Dimitrios and went without a word.

G. says that in the bedroom at that moment, when he heard the door close behind Bulic and as he held the negative up to the light, he was feeling very pleased with himself. Expenses had been low; there had been no wasted effort; there had been no tiresome delays; everybody, even Bulic, had done well out of the business. It only remained to hope that Bulic would restore the chart safely. There was really no reason why he should not do so. A very satisfactory affair from every point of view.

And then Dimitrios came into the room.

It was at that moment that G. realized that he had made one mistake.

'My wages,' said Dimitrios, and held out his hand.

G. met his employee's eyes and nodded. He needed a gun and he had not got one. 'We'll go to my house now,' he said and started towards the door.

Dimitrios shook his head deliberately. 'My wages are in your pocket.'

'Not your wages. Only mine.'

Dimitrios produced a revolver. A smile played about his lips. 'What I want is in your pocket, *mein Herr*. Put your hands behind your head.'

G. obeyed. Dimitrios walked towards him. G., looking steadily into those brown anxious eyes, saw that he was in danger. Two feet in front of him Dimitrios stopped. 'Please be careful, *mein Herr*.'

The smile disappeared. Dimitrios stepped forward suddenly and, jamming his revolver into G.'s stomach, snatched the negative from G.'s pocket with his free hand. Then, as suddenly, he stood back. 'You may go,' he said.

G. went. Dimitrios, in turn, had made *his* mistake.

All that night men, hastily recruited from the criminal cafés, scoured Belgrade for Dimitrios. But Dimitrios had disappeared. G. never saw him again.

What happened to the negative? Let me give you G.'s own words:

'When the morning came and my men had failed to find him, I knew what I must do. I felt very bitter. After all my careful work it was most disappointing. But there was nothing else for it. I had known for a week that Dimitrios had got into touch with a French agent. The negative would be in that agent's hands by now. I really had no choice. A friend of mine in the German Embassy was able to oblige me. The Germans were anxious to please Belgrade at the time. What more natural than that they should pass on an item of information interesting to the Yugoslav government?'

'Do you mean,' I said, 'that you deliberately arranged for the Yugoslav authorities to be informed of the removal of the chart and of the fact that it had been photographed?'

'Unfortunately, it was the only thing I could do. You see, I had to render the chart worthless. It was really very foolish of Dimitrios to let me go; but he was inexperienced. He probably thought that I would blackmail Bulic into bringing the chart out again. But I realized that I would not be paid much for bringing in information already in the possession of the French. Besides, my reputation would have suffered. I was very bitter about the whole affair. The only amusing aspect of it was that the French had paid over to Dimitrios half the agreed price for the chart before they discovered that the information on it had been rendered obsolete by my little *démarche*.'

'What about Bulic?'

G. pulled a face. 'Yes, I was sorry about that. I always have felt a certain responsibility towards those who work for me. He was arrested almost at once. There was no doubt as to which of the Ministry copies had been used. They were kept rolled in metal cylinders. Bulic had folded this one to bring it out of the Ministry. It was the only one with creases in it. His finger-prints did the rest. Very wisely he told the authorities all he knew about Dimitrios. As a result they sent him to prison for life instead of shooting him. I quite expected him to implicate me, but he did not. I was a little surprised. After all it was I who introduced him to Dimitrios. I wondered at the time whether it was because he was unwilling to face an additional charge of accepting bribes or because he felt grateful to me for lending him that two hundred and fifty dinar. Probably he did not connect me with the business of the chart at all. In any case, I was pleased. I still had work to do in Belgrade, and being wanted by the police, even under another name, might have complicated my life. I have never been able to bring myself to wear disguises.'

I asked him one more question. Here is his answer:

'Oh, yes, I obtained the new charts as soon as they had been made. In quite a different way, of course. With so much of my money invested in the enterprise I could not return empty-handed. It is always the same: for one reason or another there are always these delays, these wastages of effort and money. You may say that I was careless in my handling of Dimitrios. That would be unjust. It was a small error of judgment on my part, that is all. I counted on his being like all the other fools in the world, on his being too greedy; I thought he would wait until he had had from me the forty thousand dinar due to him before he tried to take the photograph as well. He took me by surprise. That error of judgment cost me a lot of money.'

'It cost Bulic his liberty.' I am afraid I said it a trifle stuffily, for he frowned.

'My dear Monsieur Latimer,' he retorted, 'Bulic was a traitor and he was rewarded according to his deserts. One cannot sentimentalize over him. In war there are always casualties. Bulic was very lucky. I would certainly have used him again, and he might ultimately have been shot. As it was, he went to prison. For all I know he is still in prison. I do not wish to seem callous, but I must say that he is better off there. His liberty? Rubbish! He had none to lose. As for his wife, I have no doubt that she has done better for herself. She always gave me the impression of wanting to do so. I do not blame her. He was an objectionable man. I seem to remember that he tended to dribble as he ate. What is more, he was a nuisance. You would have thought, would you not, that on leaving Dimitrios that evening he would have gone there and then to Alessandro to pay his debt? He did not do so. When he was arrested late the following day he still had the fifty thousand dinar in his pocket. More waste. It is at times like those, my friend, that one needs one's sense of humour.'

Well, my dear Marukakis, that is all. It is, I think, more than enough. For me, wandering among the ghosts of old lies, there is comfort in the thought that you might write to me and tell me that all this was worth finding out. You might. For myself, I begin to wonder. It is such a poor story, isn't it? There is no hero, no heroine; only villains and fools.

We shall, I hope, meet again very soon. *Croyez en mes meilleurs souvenirs.*

Charles Latimer

From a View To A Kill

FROM 'FOR YOUR EYES ONLY'

IAN FLEMING

—◆—

Ian Fleming believed that 'while thrillers may not be Literature' it was possible to write 'thrillers designed to be read as literature'.

In that aim, I think, he succeeded. True, the plots of the James Bond stories are often preposterous (Fleming himself admitted it cheerfully), but somehow that doesn't seem to matter. The author's target is not the reader's intellect but his senses; he is writing, as he put it, for 'warm-blooded heterosexuals in railway trains, airplanes or beds'; but he is doing it with style.

Moreover, in the process of entertaining us he can also inform. Where else, for example, but in 'Thunderball' are we to learn about the aphrodisiac effects of a diet of vegetable soup and weak tea, when supervised by an H-man? Where else could one find as shrewd and constructive an account of the difficulties of deciding what to drink in a Paris café as that in 'From a View To A Kill'?

Ian Fleming was a most civilized and amusing man.

—◆—

The eyes behind the wide black rubber goggles were cold as flint. In the howling speed-turmoil of his motor-bike, a BSA M20 doing seventy, they were the only quiet things in the hurtling flesh and metal. Protected by the glass of the goggles, they stared fixedly ahead from just above the centre of the handle-bars, and their dark, unwavering focus was that of gun-muzzles. Below the goggles, the wind had got into the face through the mouth and had wrenched the lips back into a square grin that showed big tombstone teeth and strips of whitish gum. On both sides of the grin the cheeks had been blown out by the wind into pouches that fluttered slightly. To right and left of the hurtling face under the crash helmet, the black gauntlets, broken-wristed at the controls, looked like the attacking paws of a big animal.

The man was dressed in the uniform of a dispatch-rider in the Royal Corps of Signals, and his machine, painted olive green, was, with certain modifications to the valves and the carburettor and the removal of some of the silencer baffles to give more speed, identical with a standard British Army machine. There was nothing in the man or his equipment to suggest that he was not what he appeared to be, except a fully loaded Luger held by a clip to the top of the petrol tank.

It was seven o'clock on a May morning, and the dead straight road through the forest glittered with the tiny luminous mist of spring. On both sides of the road the moss- and flower-carpeted depths between the great oak trees held the theatrical enchant-ment of the royal forests of Versailles and Saint-Germain. The road was D98, a secondary road serving local traffic in the Saint-Germain area, and the motor-cyclist had just passed beneath the Paris-Mantes Autoroute already thundering with commuter traffic for Paris. He was heading north toward Saint-Germain and there was no one else in sight in either direction, except, perhaps half a mile ahead, an almost identical figure—another Royal Corps dispatch-rider. He was a younger, slimmer man and he sat comfortably back on his machine, enjoying the morning and keeping his speed to around forty. He was well on time and it was a beautiful day. He wondered whether to have his eggs fried or scrambled when he got back to HQ around eight.

Five hundred yards, four hundred, three, two, one. The man coming up from behind slowed to fifty. He put his right gauntlet up to his teeth and pulled it off. He stuffed the gauntlet between the buttons of his tunic and reached down and un-clipped the gun.

By now he must have been big in the driving-mirror of the young man ahead, for suddenly the young man jerked his head around, surprised to find another dispatch-rider on his run at that time of the morning. He expected that it would be an American or perhaps French military police. It might be anyone from the eight NATO nations that made up the staff of SHAPE, but when he recognized the uniform of the Corps he was astonished and delighted. Who the hell could it be? He raised a cheerful right thumb in recognition and cut his speed to thirty, waiting for the other man to drift up alongside. With one eye on the road ahead and the other on the approach-ing silhouette in the mirror, he ran through the names of the British riders in the Special Service Transportation Unit at Headquarters Command. Albert, Sid, Wally—might be Wally, same thick build. Good show! He'd be able to pull his leg about that little frog bit in the canteen. Louise, Elise, Lise —what the hell was her name?

The man with the gun had slowed. Now he was fifty yards away. His face, undistorted by the wind, had set into blunt, hard, perhaps Slav lines. A red spark burned behind the black aimed muzzles of the eyes. Forty yards, thirty. A single magpie flew out of the forest ahead of the young dispatch-rider. It fled clumsily across the road into the bushes behind a Michelin sign that said Saint-Germain was one kilometre to go. The young man grinned and raised an ironical finger in salute and self-protection—'One magpie is sorrow'.

Twenty yards behind him the man with the gun took both hands off the handle-bars, lifted the Luger, rested it carefully on his left forearm, and fired one shot.

The young man's hands whipped off his controls and met across the centre of his backward-arching spine. His machine veered across the road, jumped a narrow ditch, and ploughed into a patch of grass and lilies of the valley. There it rose up on its screaming back wheel and slowly crashed backward on top of its dead rider. The BSA coughed and kicked and tore at the young man's clothes and at the flowers, and then lay quiet.

The killer executed a narrow turn and stopped with his machine pointing back the way he had come. He stamped down the wheel-rest, pulled his machine up on to it, and walked in among the wild flowers under the trees. He knelt down beside the dead man and brusquely pulled back an eyelid. Just as roughly he tore the black leather dispatch-case off the corpse and ripped open the buttons of the tunic and removed a battered leather wallet. He wrenched a cheap wrist watch so sharply off the left wrist that the chrome expanding bracelet snapped in half. He stood up and slung the dispatch-case over his shoulder. While he stowed the wallet and the watch away in his tunic pocket he listened. There were only forest sounds and the slow tick of hot metal from the crashed BSA. The killer retraced his steps to the road. He walked slowly, scuffing leaves over the tyre marks in the soft earth and moss. He took extra trouble over the deep scars in the ditch and the grass verge,

and then stood beside his motor-cycle and looked back toward
the lily-of-the-valley patch. Not bad! Probably only the police
dogs would get in, and, with ten miles of road to cover, they
would be hours, perhaps days—plenty long enough. The
main thing in these jobs was to have enough safety margin.
He could have shot the man at forty yards, but he had preferred
to get to twenty. And taking the watch and the wallet had been
nice touches—pro touches.

Pleased with himself, the man heaved his machine off its
rest, vaulted smartly into the saddle, and kicked down on the
starter. Slowly, so as not to show skid marks, he accelerated
away back down the road, and in a minute or so he was doing
seventy again and the wind had redrawn the empty-turnip
grin across his face.

Around the scene of the killing, the forest, which had held its
breath while it was done, slowly began to breathe again.

James Bond had his first drink of the evening at Fouquet's.
It was not a solid drink. One cannot drink seriously in French
cafés. Out of doors on a pavement in the sun is no place for
vodka or whisky or gin. A *fine à l'eau* is fairly serious, but it
intoxicates without tasting very good. A *quart de champagne*
or a *champagne à l'orange* is all right before luncheon, but in the
evening one *quart* leads to another *quart*, and a bottle of
indifferent champagne is a bad foundation for the night.
Pernod is possible, but it should be drunk in company, and anyway Bond had never liked the stuff because its liquorice taste reminded him of his childhood. No, in cafés you have to drink the
least offensive of the musical-comedy drinks that go with them,
and Bond always had the same thing, an Americano—bitter
Campari, Cinzano, a large slice of lemon peel, and soda. For the
soda he always stipulated Perrier, for in his opinion expensive

soda water was the cheapest way to improve a poor drink. When Bond was in Paris he invariably stuck to the same addresses. He stayed at the Terminus Nord, because he liked station hotels and because this was the least pretentious and most anonymous of them. He had luncheon at the Café de la Paix, the Rotonde, or the Dôme, because the food was good enough and it amused him to watch the people. If he wanted a solid drink he had it at Harry's Bar, both because of the solidity of the drinks and because, on his first ignorant visit to Paris at the age of sixteen, he had done what Harry's advertisement in the *Continental Daily Mail* had told him to do and had said to his taxi-driver, 'Sank Roo Doe Noo'. That had started one of the memorable evenings of his life, culminating in the loss, almost simultaneous, of his virginity and his note-case. For dinner, Bond went to one of the great restaurants— Véfour, the Caneton, Lucas-Carton, or the Cochon d'Or. These he considered, whatever Michelin might say about the Tour d'Argent, Maxim's, and the like, to have somehow avoided the tarnish of the expense account and the dollar. Anyway, he preferred their cooking. After dinner he generally went to the Place Pigalle to see what would happen to him. When, as usual, nothing did, he would walk home across Paris to the Gare du Nord and go to bed.

To-night Bond decided to tear up this dusty address book and have himself an old-fashioned ball. He was on his way through Paris after a dismally failed assignment on the Austro-Hungarian border. It had been a question of getting a certain Hungarian out. Bond had been sent from London specially to direct the operation over the head of Station V. This had been unpopular with the Vienna Station. There had been mis-understandings—wilful ones. The man had been killed in the frontier minefield. There would have to be a Court of Inquiry.

Bond was due back at his London headquarters on the following day to make his report, and the thought of it all depressed him. To-day had been so beautiful—one of those days when you almost believe that Paris is beautiful and gay—and Bond had decided to give the town just one more chance. He would somehow find himself a girl who was a real girl, and he would take her to dinner at some make-believe place in the Bois like the Armenonville. To clean the money-look out of her eyes— for it would certainly be there—he would as soon as possible give her fifty thousand francs. He would say to her, 'I propose to call you Donatienne, or possibly Solange, because these are names that suit my mood and the evening. We knew each other before and you lent me this money because I was in a jam. Here it is, and now we will tell each other what we have been doing since we last met in Saint-Tropez just a year ago. In the meantime, here is the menu and the wine list and you must choose what will make you happy and fat.' And she would look relieved at not having to try any more, and she would laugh and say, 'But, James, I do not want to be fat.' And there they would be, started on the myth of 'Paris in the Spring', and Bond would stay sober and be interested in her and everything she said. And, by God, by the end of the evening it would not be his fault if it transpired that there was in fact no shred of stuffing left in that hoary old fairy tale of 'A good time in Paris'.

Sitting in Fouquet's, waiting for his Americano, Bond smiled at his vehemence. He knew that he was only playing at fantasy for the satisfaction of launching a last kick at a town he had cordially disliked since the war. Since 1945, he had not had a happy day in Paris. It was not that the town had sold its body. Many towns have done that. It was its heart that was gone— pawned to the tourists, pawned to the Russians and Rumanians and Bulgars, pawned to the scum of the world who had gradually taken the town over. And, of course, pawned to the Germans. You could see it in the people's eyes—sullen, envious, ashamed. Architecture? Bond glanced across the pavement at the shiny black ribbons of cars off which the sun glinted painfully. Everywhere it was the same as in the Champs-Elysées. There were only two hours in which you could even see the town—between five and seven in the morning. After seven it was engulfed in a thundering stream of black metal with which no beautiful buildings, no spacious, tree-lined boulevards, could compete.

The waiter's tray clattered down on the marble-topped table. With a slick one-handed jerk that Bond had never been able to copy, the waiter's bottle-opener prised the cap off the Perrier. The man slipped the tab under the icebucket, said a mechanical, '*Voilà, m'sieur*,' and darted away. Bond put ice into his drink, filled it to the top with soda, and took a long pull at it. He sat back and lit a Laurens *jaune*. Of course the evening would be a disaster. Even supposing he found the girl in the next hour or so, the contents would certainly not stand up to the wrapping. On closer examination she would turn out to have the heavy, dank, wide-pored skin of the bourgeois French. The blond hair under the rakish velvet beret would be brown at the roots and as coarse as piano wire. The peppermint on the breath would not conceal the midday garlic. The alluring figure would be intricately scaffolded with wire and rubber. She would be from Lille and she would ask him if he was American. And—Bond smiled to himself—she or her *maquereau* would probably steal his notecase. *La ronde!* He would be back where he came in. More or less, that was. Well, to hell with it!

A battered black Peugeot 403 broke out of the centre stream of traffic, cut across the inside line of cars, and pulled in to double park at the kerb. There was the usual screaming of

brakes, hooting, and yelling. Quite unmoved, a girl got out of
the car and, leaving the traffic to sort itself out, walked purpose-
fully across the pavement. Bond sat up. She had everything,
but absolutely everything that belonged in his fantasy. She
was tall and, although her figure was hidden by a light raincoat,
the way she moved and the way she held herself promised that
it would be beautiful. The face had the gaiety and bravado that
went with her driving, but now there was impatience in the
compressed lips and the eyes fretted as she pushed diagonally
through the moving crowd on the pavement.

Bond watched her narrowly as she reached the edge of the
tables and came up the aisle. Of course it was hopeless. She
was coming to meet someone—her lover. She was the sort of
woman who always belongs to somebody else. She was late
for him. That's why she was in such a hurry. What damnable
luck—right down to the long blond hair under the rakish
beret! And she was looking straight at him. She was
smiling . . . !

Before Bond could pull himself together, the girl had come
up to his table and had drawn out a chair and sat down.

She smiled rather tautly into his startled eyes. 'I'm sorry
I'm late, and I'm afraid we've got to get moving at once. You're
wanted at the office.' She added under her breath, 'Crash dive.'

Bond jerked himself back to reality. Whoever she was, she
was certainly from 'the firm'. 'Crash dive' was a slang expression the Secret Service had borrowed from the Submarine
Service. It meant bad news—the worst. Bond dug into his
pockets and slid some coins over the tab. He said, 'Right.
Let's go', and got up and followed her down through the tables
and across to her car. It was still obstructing the inner lane of
traffic. Any minute now there would be a policeman. Angry
faces glared at them as they climbed in. The girl had left the

engine running. She banged the gears into second and slid out into the traffic.

Bond looked sideways at her. The pale skin was velvet. The blond hair was silk—to the roots. He said, 'Where are you from and what's it all about?'

She said, concentrating on the traffic, 'From the Station. Grade two assistant. Number 765 on duty, Mary Ann Russell off. I've no idea what it's all about. I just saw the signal from HQ—personal from M to Head of Station. Most Immediate and all that. He was to find you at once and if necessary use the Deuxième to help. Head of F said you always went to the same places when you were in Paris, and I and another girl were given a list.' She smiled. 'I'd only tried Harry's Bar, and after Fouquet's I was going to start on the restaurants. It was marvellous picking you up like that.' She gave him a quick glance. 'I hope I wasn't very clumsy.'

Bond said, 'You were fine. How were you going to handle it if I'd had a girl with me?'

She laughed. 'I was going to do much the same except call you "sir". I was only worried about how you'd dispose of the girl. If she started a scene I was going to offer to take her home in my car and for you to take a taxi.'

'You sound pretty resourceful. How long have you been in the Service?'

'Five years. This is my first time with a station.'

'How do you like it?'

'I like the work all right. The evenings and days off drag a bit. It's not easy to make friends in Paris without'—her mouth turned down with irony—'without all the rest. I mean,' she hastened to add, 'I'm not a prude and all that, but somehow the French make the whole business such a bore. I mean I've had to give up taking the Métro or buses. Whatever time of day it is, you end up with your behind black and blue.' She laughed. 'Apart from the boredom of it and not knowing what to say to the man, some of the pinches really hurt. It's the limit. So to get around I bought this car cheap, and other cars seem to keep out of my way. As long as you don't catch the other driver's eye, you can take on even the meanest of them. They're afraid you haven't seen them. And they're worried by the bashed-about look of the car. They give you a wide berth.'

They had come to the Rond Point. As if to demonstrate her theory, she tore round it and went straight at the line of traffic coming up from the Place de la Concorde. Miraculously it divided and let her through into the Avenue Matignon.

Bond said, 'Pretty good. But don't make it a habit. There may be some French Mary Anns about.'

She laughed. She turned into the Avenue Gabrielle and pulled up outside the Paris headquarters of the Secret Service. 'I only try that sort of manoeuvre in the line of duty.'

Bond got out and came round to her side of the car. He said, 'Well, thanks for picking me up. When this whirl is over, can I pick you up in exchange? I don't get the pinches, but I'm just as bored in Paris as you are.'

Her eyes were blue and wide apart. They searched his. She said seriously, 'I'd like that. The switchboard here can always find me.'

Bond reached in through the window and pressed the hand on the wheel. He said, 'Good', and turned and walked quickly in through the archway.

Wing Commander Rattray, Head of Station F, was a fattish man with pink cheeks and fair hair brushed straight back. He dressed in a mannered fashion with turned-back cuffs and double slits to his coat, bow ties and fancy waistcoats. He made a good-living, wine-and-food-society impression in which only the slow, rather cunning blue eyes struck a false note. He chain-smoked Gauloises and his office stank of them. He greeted Bond with relief. 'Who found you?'

'Russell. At Fouquet's. Is she new?'

'Six months. She's a good one. But take a pew. There's the hell of a flap on and I've got to brief you and get you going.' He bent to his intercom and pressed down a switch. 'Signal to M, please. Personal from Head of Station. "Located 007 briefing now." Okay?' He let go the switch.

Bond pulled a chair over by the open window to keep away from the fog of Gauloise. The traffic on the Champs-Elysées was a soft roar in the background. Half an hour before he had been fed up with Paris, glad to be going. Now he hoped he would be staying.

Head of F said, 'Somebody got our dawn dispatch-rider from SHAPE to the Saint-Germain Station yesterday morning. The weekly run from the SHAPE Intelligence Division with the Summaries, Joint Intelligence papers, Iron Curtain Order of Battle—all the top gen. One shot in the back. Took his dispatch-case and his wallet and watch.'

Bond said, 'That's bad. No chance that it was an ordinary hold-up? Or do they think the wallet and watch were cover?'

'SHAPE Security can't make up their minds. On the whole they guess it was cover. Seven o'clock in the morning's a rum time for a hold-up. But you can argue it out with them when you get down there. M's sending you as his personal representative. He's worried as hell. Apart from the loss of the Intelligence dope, their I. people have never liked having one of our stations outside the reservation, so to speak. For years they've been trying to get the Saint-Germain unit incorporated in the SHAPE Intelligence set-up. But you know what M is, independent old devil. He's never been happy about NATO Security.

Why, right in the SHAPE Intelligence Division there are not only a couple of Frenchmen and an Italian, but the head of their Counterintelligence and Security section is a German!'

Bond whistled.

'The trouble is that this damnable business is all SHAPE needs to bring M to heel. Anyway, he says you're to get down there right away. I've fixed up clearance for you. Got the passes. You're to report to Colonel Schreiber, Headquarters Command Security Branch. American. Efficient chap. He's been handling the thing from the beginning. As far as I can gather, he's already done just about all there was to be done.'

'What's he done? What actually happened?'

Head of F picked up a map from his desk and walked over with it. It was the big-scale Michelin *Environs de Paris*. He pointed with a pencil. 'Here's Versailles, and here, just north of the park, is the big junction of the Paris-Mantes and the Versailles Autoroutes. A couple of hundred yards north of that, on N184, is SHAPE. Every Wednesday, at seven in the morning, a Special Services dispatch-rider leaves SHAPE with the weekly Intelligence stuff I told you about. He has to get to this little village called Fourqueux, just outside Saint-Germain, deliver his stuff to the duty officer at our HQ, and report back to SHAPE by seven-thirty. Rather than go through all this built-up area, for security reasons his orders are to take this N307 to Saint-Nom, turn right-handed on to D98, and go under the Autoroute and through the Forest of Saint-Germain. The distance is about twelve kilometres, and, taking it easy, he'll do the trip in under a quarter of an hour. Well, yesterday it was a corporal from the Corps of Signals, good solid man called Bates, and when he hadn't reported back to SHAPE by seven-forty-five they sent another rider to look for him. Not a trace, and he hadn't reported at our HQ. By eight-fifteen the Security

Branch was on the job, and by nine the roadblocks were up. The police and the Deuxième were told and search parties got under way. The dogs found him but not till the evening around six, and by that time if there had been any clues on the road they'd been wiped out by the traffic.' Head of F handed the map to Bond and walked back to his desk. 'And that's about the lot, except that all the usual steps have been taken—frontiers, ports, aerodromes and so forth. But that sort of thing won't help. If it was a professional job, whoever did it could have had the stuff out of the country by midday or into an embassy in Paris inside an hour.'

Bond said impatiently, 'Exactly! And so what the hell does M expect me to do? Tell SHAPE Security to do it all over again, but better? This sort of thing isn't my line at all. Bloody waste of time.'

Head of F smiled sympathetically. 'Matter of fact I put much the same point of view to M over the scrambler. Tactfully. The old man was quite reasonable. Said he wanted to show SHAPE he was taking the business just as seriously as they were. You happened to be available and more or less on the spot, and he said you had the sort of mind that might pick up the invisible factor. I asked him what he meant, and he said that at all closely guarded headquarters there's bound to be an invisible man, a man everyone takes so much for granted that he just isn't noticed—gardener, window-cleaner, postman. I said that SHAPE had thought of that, and that all those sort of jobs were done by enlisted men. M told me not to be so literal-minded and hung up.'

Bond laughed. He could see M's frown and hear the crusty voice. He said, 'All right, then. I'll see what I can do. Who do I report back to?'

'Here. M doesn't want the Saint-Germain unit to get in-

volved. Anything you have to say I'll put straight on the printer
to London. But I may not be available when you call up. I'll
make someone your duty officer and you'll be able to get them
at any time in the twenty-four hours. Russell can do it. She
picked you up. She might as well carry you. Suit you?'

'Yes,' said Bond. 'That'll be all right.'

The battered Peugeot, commandeered by Rattray, smelled of
her. There were bits of her in the glove compartment—half a
packet of Suchard milk chocolate, a twist of paper containing
bobby pins, a paperback John O'Hara, a single black suede
glove. Bond thought about her as far as the Etoile and then
closed his mind to her and pushed the car along fast through the
Bois. Rattray had said it would take about fifteen minutes at
fifty. Bond said to halve the speed and double the time and to
tell Colonel Schreiber that he would be with him by nine-
thirty. After the Porte de Saint-Cloud there was little traffic,
and Bond held seventy on the Autoroute until the second exit
road came up on his right and there was the red arrow for
SHAPE. Bond turned up the slope and on to N184. Two hundred
yards farther, in the centre of the road, was the traffic policeman Bond had been told to look out for. The policeman waved
him in through the big gates on the left and he pulled up at the
first checkpoint. A grey-uniformed American policeman hung
out of the cabin and glanced at his pass. He was told to pull
inside and hold it. Now a French policeman took his pass,
noted the details on a printed form clipped to a board, gave
him a large plastic windshield number, and waved him on.
As Bond pulled into the car park, with theatrical suddenness a
hundred arc-lights blazed and lit up the acre of low-lying
hutments in front of him as if it were day. Feeling naked,
Bond walked across the open gravel beneath the flags of the
NATO countries and ran up the four shallow steps to the wide

glass doors that gave entrance to the Supreme Headquarters Allied Forces Europe. Now there was the main Security desk. American and French military police again checked his pass and noted the details. He was handed over to a red-capped British MP and led off down the main corridor past endless office doors. They bore no names but the usual alphabetical abracadabra of all headquarters. One said COMSTRIKFLTLANT AND SACLANT LIAISON TO SACEUR. Bond asked what it meant. The military policeman, either ignorant or, more probably, security-minded, said stolidly, 'Couldn't rightly say, sir.'

Behind a door that said COLONEL G. A. SCHREIBER, CHIEF OF SECURITY, HEADQUARTERS COMMAND, was a ramrod-straight middle-aged American with greying hair and the politely negative manner of a bank manager. There were several family photographs in silver frames on his desk and a vase containing one white rose. There was no smell of tobacco smoke in the room. After cautiously amiable preliminaries, Bond congratulated the colonel on his security. He said, 'All these checks and double checks don't make it easy for the opposition. Have you ever lost anything before, or have you ever found signs of a serious attempt at a *coup*?'

'No to both questions, Commander. I'm quite satisfied about Headquarters. It's only the outlying units that worry me. Apart from this section of your Secret Service, we have various detached signal units. Then, of course, there are the Home Ministries of fourteen different nations. I can't answer for what may leak from those quarters.'

'It can't be an easy job,' agreed Bond. 'Now, about this mess. Has anything else come up since Wing Commander Rattray spoke to you last?'

'Got the bullet. Luger. Severed the spinal cord. Probably fired at around thirty yards, give or take ten yards. Assuming our man was riding a straight course, the bullet must have been fired from dead astern on a level trajectory. Since it can't have been a man standing in the road, the killer must have been moving in or on some vehicle.'

'So your man would have seen him in the driving-mirror?'

'Probably.'

'If your riders find themselves being followed, do they have any instructions about taking evasive action?'

The colonel smiled lightly. 'Sure. They're told to go like hell.'

'And at what speed did your man crash?'

'Not fast, they think. Between twenty and forty. What are you getting at, Commander?'

'I was wondering if you'd decided whether it was a pro or an amateur job. If your man wasn't trying to get away, and assuming he saw the killer in his mirror, which I agree is only a probability, that suggests that he accepted the man on his tail as friend rather than foe. That could mean some sort of a disguise that would fit in with the set-up here—something your man would accept even at that hour of the morning.'

A small frown had been gathering across Colonel Schreiber's smooth forehead. 'Commander'—there was an edge of tension in the voice—'we have, of course, been considering every angle of this case, including the one you mention. At midday yesterday the commanding general declared emergency in this matter, standing security and security ops committees were set up, and from that moment on every angle, every hint of a clue, has been systematically run to earth. And I can tell you, Commander'—the colonel raised one well-manicured hand and let it descend in soft emphasis on his blotting-pad—'any man who can come up with an even remotely original idea on this case will have to be closely related to Einstein. There is nothing, repeat nothing, to go on in this case whatsoever.'

Bond smiled sympathetically. He got to his feet. 'In that case, Colonel, I won't waste any more of your time this evening. If I could just have the minutes of the various meetings to bring myself up to date, and if one of your men could show me the way to the canteen and my quarters . . .'

'Sure, sure.' The colonel pressed a bell. A young crew-cutted aide came in. 'Proctor, show the commander to his room in the VIP wing, would you, and then take him along to the bar and the canteen.' He turned to Bond. 'I'll have those papers ready for you after you've had a meal and a drink. They'll be in my office. They can't be taken out, of course, but you'll find everything to hand next door, and Proctor will be able to fill you in on anything that's missing.' He held out his hand. 'Okay? Then we'll meet again in the morning.'

Bond said good night and followed the aide out. As he walked along the neutral-painted, neutral-smelling corridors, he reflected that this was probably the most hopeless assignment he had ever been on. If the top security brains of fourteen countries were stumped, what hope had he got? By the time he was in bed that night, in the Spartan luxury of the visitors' overnight quarters, Bond had decided he would give it a couple more days —largely for the sake of keeping in touch with Mary Ann Russell for as long as possible—and then chuck it. On this decision he fell immediately into a deep and untroubled sleep.

Not two but four days later, as the dawn come up over the Forest of Saint-Germain, James Bond was lying along the thick branch of an oak tree, keeping watch over a small empty glade that lay deep among the trees bordering D98, the road of the murder.

He was dressed from head to foot in parachutists' camouflage—green, brown, and black. Even his hands were covered with the stuff, and there was a hood over his head with slits

cut for the eyes and mouth. It was good camouflage, which
would be still better when the sun was higher and the shadows
blacker, and from anywhere on the ground, even directly
below the high branch, he could not be seen.

It had come about like this. The first two days at SHAPE had
been the expected waste of time. Bond had achieved nothing
except to make himself mildly unpopular with the persistence
of his double-checking questions. On the morning of the third
day he was about to go and say his good-byes when he had a
telephone call from the colonel. 'Oh, Commander, thought I'd
let you know that the last team of police dogs got in late last
night—your idea that it might be worth while covering the
whole forest. Sorry'—the voice sounded unsorry—'but
negative, absolutely negative.'

'Oh. My fault for the wasted time.' As much to annoy the
colonel as anything, Bond said, 'Mind if I have a talk with the
handler?'

'Sure, sure. Anything you want. By the way, Commander,
how long are you planning to be around? Glad to have you
with us for as long as you like. But it's a question of your room.
Seems there's a big party coming in from Holland in a few
days' time. Top-level staff course or something of the kind,
and Admin says they're a bit pushed for space.'

Bond had not expected to get on well with Colonel Schreiber
and he had not done so. He said amiably, 'I'll see what my
chief has to say and call you back, Colonel.'

'Do that, would you.' The Colonel's voice was equally polite,
but the manners of both men were running out and the two
receivers broke the line simultaneously.

The chief handler was a Frenchman from the Landes. He
had the quick, sly eyes of a poacher. Bond met him at the
kennels, but the handler's proximity was too much for the

Alsatians, and to get away from the noise he took Bond into the duty-room, a tiny office with binoculars hanging from pegs, and waterproofs, gumboots, dog-harness, and other gear stacked round the walls. There were a couple of deal chairs and a table covered with a large-scale map of the Forest of Saint-Germain. This had been marked off into pencilled squares. The handler made a gesture over the map. 'Our dogs covered it all, monsieur. There is nothing there.'

'Do you mean to say they didn't check once?'

The handler scratched his head. 'We had trouble with a bit of game, monsieur. There was a hare or two. A couple of foxes' earths. We had quite a time getting them away from a clearing near the Carrefour Royal. They probably still smelled the gypsies.'

'Oh.' Bond was only mildly interested. 'Show me. Who were these gypsies?'

The handler pointed daintily with a grimy little finger. 'These are the names from the old days. Here is the Etoile Parfaite, and here, where the killing took place, is the Carrefour des Curieux. And here, forming the bottom of the triangle, is the Carrefour Royal. It makes,' he added dramatically, 'a cross with the road of death.' He took a pencil out of his pocket and made a dot just off the cross roads. 'And this is the clearing, monsieur. There was a gypsy caravan there for most of the winter. They left last month. Cleaned the place up all right, but, for the dogs, their scent will hang about there for months.'

Bond thanked him and, after inspecting and admiring the dogs and making some small talk about the handler's profession, he got into the Peugeot and went off to the *gendarmerie* in Saint-Germain. Yes, certainly they had known the gypsies. Real Romany-looking fellows. Hardly spoke a word of French, but they had behaved themselves. There had been no complaints. Six men and two women. No. No one had seen them go. One morning they just weren't there any more. Might have been gone a week for all one knew. They had chosen an isolated spot.

Bond took the D98 through the forest. When the great Autoroute bridge showed up a quarter of a mile ahead over the road, Bond accelerated and then switched off the engine and coasted silently until he came to the Carrefour Royal. He stopped and got out of the car without a sound, and, feeling rather foolish, softly entered the forest and walked with great circumspection toward where the clearing would be. Twenty yards inside the trees he came to it. He stood in the fringe of bushes and trees and examined it carefully. Then he walked in and went over it from end to end.

The clearing was about as big as two tennis courts and floored in thick grass and moss. There was one large patch of lilies of the valley and, under the bordering trees, a scattering of bluebells. To one side there was a low mound, perhaps a tumulus, completely surrounded and covered with brambles and brier roses now thickly in bloom. Bond walked round this and gazed in among the roots, but there was nothing to see except the earthy shape of the mound.

Bond took one last look around and then went to the corner of the clearing that would be nearest to the road. Here there was easy access through the trees. Were there traces of a path, a slight flattening of the leaves? Not more than would have been left by the gypsies or last year's picnickers. On the edge of the road there was a narrow passage between two trees. Casually Bond bent to examine the trunks. He stiffened and dropped to a crouch. With a fingernail he delicately scraped away a narrow sliver of caked mud. It hid a deep scratch in the tree-trunk. He caught the scraps of mud in his free hand. He now spat and moistened the mud and carefully filled up the scratch again. There were three camouflaged scratches on one tree and four on the other. Bond walked quickly out of the trees on to the road. His car had stopped on a slight slope leading down under the Autoroute bridge. Although there was some protection from the boom of the traffic on the Autoroute, Bond pushed the car, jumped in, and engaged the gears only when he was well under the bridge.

And now Bond was back in the clearing, above it, and he still did not know if his hunch had been right. It had been M's dictum that had put him on the scent—if it was a scent—and the mention of the gypsies. 'It was the gypsies the dogs smelled ... Most of the winter ... they went last month. No complaints ... One morning they just weren't there any more.' The invisible factor. The invisible man. The people who are so much part of the background that you don't know if they're there or not. Six men and two girls, and they hardly spoke a word of French. Good cover, gypsies. You could be a foreigner and yet not a foreigner, because you were only a gypsy. Some of them had gone off in the caravan. Had some of them stayed, built themselves a hide-out during the winter, a secret place from which the hijacking of the top-secret dispatches had been the first sortie? Bond had thought he was building fantasies until he found the scratches, the carefully camouflaged scratches, on the two trees. They were just at the height where, if one was carrying any kind of cycle, the pedals might catch against the bark. It could all be a pipedream, but it was good enough for Bond. The only question in his mind was whether these people had made a one-time-only coup or whether they were so confident of their security that they would try again. He confided only in Station F. Mary Ann Russell told him to be careful. Head of F, more constructively, ordered his unit at Saint-Germain to co-operate. Bond said good-bye to Colonel

Schreiber and moved to a camp-bed in the unit's HQ—an
anonymous house in an anonymous village back street. The
unit had provided the camouflage outfit, and the four Secret
Service men who ran the unit had happily put themselves under
Bond's orders. They realized as well as Bond did that if Bond
managed to wipe the eye of the whole security machine of
SHAPE, the Secret Service would have won a priceless feather
in its cap *vis-à-vis* the SHAPE high command, and M's worries
over the independence of his unit would be gone forever.

Bond, lying along the oak branch, smiled to himself. Private
armies, private wars. How much energy they siphoned off from
the common cause, how much fire they directed away from the
common enemy!

Six-thirty. Time for breakfast. Cautiously Bond's right hand
fumbled in his clothing and came up to the slit of his mouth.
Bond made the glucose tablet last as long as possible and then
sucked another. His eyes never left the glade. The red squirrel
that had appeared at first light and had been steadily eating
away at young beech shoots ever since ran a few feet nearer to
the rose bushes on the mound, picked up something, and began
turning it in its paws and nibbling at it. Two wood-pigeons
that had been noisily courting among the thick grass started to
make clumsy, fluttering love. A pair of hedge-sparrows went
busily on collecting bits and pieces for a nest they were tardily
building in a thorn bush. The fat thrush finally located its
worm and began pulling at it, legs braced. Bees clustered thick
among the roses on the mound, and from where he was,
perhaps twenty yards away from and above the mound, Bond
could just hear their summery sound. It was a scene from a fairy
tale—the roses, the lilies of the valley, the birds, and the great
shafts of sunlight lancing down through the tall trees into the
pool of glistening green. Bond had climbed to his hide-out at

four in the morning and he had never examined so closely or for so long the transition from night to a glorious day. He suddenly felt rather foolish. Any moment now and some damned bird would come and sit on his head!

It was the pigeons that gave the first alarm. With a loud clatter they took off and dashed into the trees. All the birds followed, and the squirrel. Now the glade was quite quiet except for the soft hum of the bees. What had sounded the alarm? Bond's heart began to thump. His eyes hunted, quartering the glade for a clue. Something was moving among the roses. It was a tiny movement, but an extraordinary one. Slowly, inch by inch, a single thorny stem, an unnaturally straight and rather thick one, was rising through the upper branches. It went on rising until it was a clear foot above the bush. Then it stopped. There was a solitary pink rose at the tip of the stem. Separated from the bush, it looked unnatural but only if one happened to have watched the whole process. at a casual glance it was a stray stem and nothing else. Now, silently, the petals of the rose seemed to swivel and expand, the yellow pistils drew aside, and sun glinted on a glass lens the size of a shilling. The lens seemed to be looking straight at Bond, but then very, very slowly, the rose-eye began to turn on its stem and continued to turn until the lens was again looking at Bond and the whole glade had been minutely surveyed. As if satisfied, the petals softly swivelled to cover the eye, and very slowly the single rose descended to join the others.

Bond's breath came out with a rush. He momentarily closed his eyes to rest them. Gypsies! If that piece of machinery was any evidence, inside the mound, deep down in the earth, was certainly the most professional left-behind spy unit that had ever been devised, far more brilliant than anything England had prepared to operate in the wake of a successful German invasion, far better than what the Germans themselves had left behind in the Ardennes. A shiver of excitement and anticipation—almost of fear—ran down Bond's spine. So he had been right! But what was to be the next act?

Now, from the direction of the mound, came a thin, high-pitched whine, the sound of an electric motor at very high revs. The rose bush trembled slightly. The bees took off, hovered, and settled again. Slowly a jagged fissure formed down the centre of the big bush and smoothly widened. Now the two halves of the bush were opening like double doors. The dark aperture broadened until Bond could see the roots of the bush running into earth on both sides of the opening doorway. The whine of machinery was louder, and there was a glint of metal from the edges of the curved doors. It was like the opening of a hinged Easter egg. In a moment the two segments stood apart and the two halves of the rose bush, still alive with bees, were splayed wide open. Now the inside of the metal caisson that supported the earth and the roots of the bush was naked to the sun. There was a glint of pale electric light from the dark aperture between the curved doors. The whine of the motor had stopped. A head and shoulders appeared, and then the rest of the man. He climbed softly out and crouched, looking sharply round the glade. There was a gun—a Luger—in his hand. Satisfied, he turned and gestured into the shaft. The head and shoulders of a second man appeared. He handed up three pairs of what looked like snowshoes and ducked out of sight. The first man selected a pair and knelt and strapped them over his boots. Now he moved about more freely, leaving no footprints, for the grass flattened only momentarily under the wide mesh and then rose slowly again. Bond smiled to himself. Clever bastards!

The second man emerged. He was followed by a third.

Between them they manhandled a motor-cycle out of the shaft and stood holding it slung between them by harness webbing while the first man, who was clearly the leader, knelt and strapped the snowshoes under their boots. Then, in single file, they moved off through the trees toward the road. There was something extraordinarily sinister about the way they softly high-stepped along through the shadows, lifting and carefully placing each big webbed foot in turn.

Bond let out a long sigh of released tension and laid his head softly down on the branch to relax the strain in his neck muscles. So that was the score! Even the last small detail could now be added to the file. While the two underlings were dressed in grey overalls, the leader was wearing the uniform of the Royal Corps of Signals, and his motor-cycle was an olive-green BSA M20 with a British Army registration number on its petrol tank. No wonder the SHAPE dispatch-rider had let him get within range. And what did the unit do with its top-secret booty? Probably radioed the cream of it out at night. Instead of the periscope, a rose-stalked aerial would rise up from the bush, the pedal generator would get going deep down under the earth, and off would go the high-speed cipher groups. Ciphers? There would be many good enemy secrets down that shaft if Bond could round up the unit when it was outside the hide-out. And what a chance to feed back phoney intelligence to GRU, the Soviet Military Intelligence Apparat, which was presumably the control! Bond's thoughts raced.

The two underlings were coming back. They went into the shaft, and the rose bush closed over it. The leader with his machine would be among the bushes on the verge of the road. Bond glanced at his watch. Six-fifty-five. Of course! He would be waiting to see if a dispatch-rider came along. Either he did not know the man he had killed was doing a weekly run, which was unlikely, or he was assuming that SHAPE would now change the routine for additional security. These were careful people. Probably their orders were to clean up as much as possible before the summer came and there were too many holiday-makers about in the forest. Then the unit might be pulled out and put back again in the winter. Who could say what the long-term plans were? Sufficient that the leader was preparing for another kill.

The minutes ticked by. At seven-ten the leader reappeared. He stood in the shadow of a big tree at the edge of the clearing and whistled once on a brief, high, bird-like note. Immediately the rose bush began to open and the two underlings came out and followed the leader back into the trees. In two minutes they were back with the motor-cycle slung between them. The leader, after a careful look around to see that they had left no traces, followed them down into the shaft, and the two halves of the rose bush closed swiftly behind him.

Half an hour later life had started up in the glade again. An hour later still, when the high sun had darkened the shadows, James Bond silently edged backward along his branch, dropped softly on to a patch of moss behind some brambles, and melted carefully back into the forest.

That evening Bond's routine call to Mary Ann Russell was a stormy one. She said, 'You're crazy. I'm not going to let you do it. I'm going to get Head of F to ring up Colonel Schreiber and tell him the whole story. This is SHAPE's job. Not yours.'

Bond said sharply, 'You'll do nothing of the sort. Colonel Schreiber says he's perfectly happy to let me make a dummy run to-morrow morning instead of the duty dispatch-rider. That's all he needs to know at this stage. Reconstruction of the crime sort of thing. He couldn't care less. He's practically closed the file on this business. Now, be a good girl and do as you're told. Just put my report on the printer to M. He'll see the point of me cleaning this thing up. He won't object.'

'Damn M! Damn you! Damn the whole silly Service!' There were angry tears in the voice. 'You're just a lot of children playing at Red Indians. Taking these people on by yourself. It's—it's showing off. That's all it is. Showing off.'

Bond was beginning to get annoyed. He said, 'That's enough, Mary Ann. Put that report on the printer. I'm sorry, but it's an order.'

There was resignation in the voice. 'Oh, all right. You don't have to pull your rank on me. But don't get hurt. At least you'll have the boys from the local Station to pick up the bits. Good luck.'

'Thanks, Mary Ann. And will you have dinner with me tomorrow night? Some place like Armenonville. Pink champagne and gypsy violins. Paris-in-the-spring routine.'

'Yes,' she said seriously. 'I'd like that. But then take care all the more, would you? Please?'

'Of course I will. Don't worry. Good night.'

'Night.'

Bond spent the rest of the evening putting a last high polish on his plans and giving a final briefing to the four men from the Station.

It was another beautiful day. Bond, sitting comfortably astride the throbbing BSA waiting for the take-off, could hardly believe in the ambush that would now be waiting for him just beyond the Carrefour Royal. The corporal from the Signal Corps who had handed him his empty dispatch-case and was about to give him the signal to go said, 'You look as if you'd been in the Royal Corps all your life, sir. Time for a haircut soon, I'd say, but the uniform's bang on. How d'you like the bike, sir?'

'Goes like a dream. I'd forgotten what fun these damned things are.'

'Give me a nice little Austin A40 any day, sir.' The corporal looked at his watch. 'Seven o'clock just coming up.' He held up his thumb. 'Okay.'

Bond pulled the goggles down over his eyes, lifted a hand to the corporal, kicked the machine into gear, and wheeled off across the gravel and through the main gates.

Off 184 and on to 307, through Bailly and Noisy-le-Roi, and there was the straggle of Saint-Nom. Here he would be turning sharp right on to D98—*the route de la mort*, as the handler had called it. Bond pulled in to the grass verge and once more looked to the long-barrel ·45 Colt. He put the warm gun back against his stomach and left the jacket button undone. On your marks! Get set . . . !

Bond took the sharp corner and accelerated up to fifty. The viaduct carrying the Paris Autoroute loomed up ahead. The dark mouth of the tunnel beneath it opened and swallowed him. The noise of his exhaust was gigantic, and for an instant there was a tunnel smell of cold and damp. Then he was out in the sunshine again and immediately across the Carrefour Royal. Ahead the oily tarmac glittered dead straight for two miles through the enchanted forest, and there was a sweet smell of leaves and dew. Bond cut his speed to forty. The driving-mirror by his left hand shivered lightly with his speed. It showed nothing but an empty unfurling vista of road between lines of trees that curled away behind him like a green wake. No sign of the killer. Had he taken fright? Had there been some hitch? But then there was a tiny black speck in the centre of the convex glass—a midge that became a fly and then a bee and then a beetle. Now it was a crash helmet bent low over handle-bars between two big black paws. God, he was coming fast! Bond's eyes flickered from the mirror to the road ahead and back to the mirror. When the killer's right hand went for his gun . . . !

Bond slowed—thirty-five, thirty, twenty. Ahead the tarmac was smooth as metal. A last quick look in the mirror. The right hand had left the handlebars. The sun on the man's goggles made huge fiery eyes below the rim of the crash helmet. Now! Bond braked fiercely and skidded the BSA through forty-five degrees, killing the engine. He was not quite quick enough on the draw. The killer's gun flared twice, and a bullet tore into the saddle-springs beside Bond's thigh. But then the Colt spoke its single word, and the killer and his BSA, as if lassoed from within the forest, veered crazily off the road, leaped the ditch, and crashed head on into the trunk of a beech. For a moment the tangle of man and machinery clung to the broad trunk, and then, with a metallic death-rattle, toppled backward into the grass.

Bond got off his machine and walked over to the ugly twist of khaki and smoking steel. There was no need to feel for a pulse. Wherever the bullet had struck, the crash helmet had smashed like an eggshell. Bond turned away and thrust his gun back into the front of his tunic. He had been lucky. It would not do to press his luck. He got on the BSA and accelerated back down the road.

He leaned the BSA up against one of the scarred trees just inside the forest and walked softly through to the edge of the clearing. He took up his stand in the shadow of the big beech. He moistened his lips and gave, as near as he could, the killer's bird-whistle. He waited. Had he got the whistle wrong? But then the bush trembled and the high, thin whine began. Bond hooked his right thumb through his belt within inches of his gun-butt. He hoped he would not have to do any more killing. The two underlings had not seemed to be armed. With any luck they would come quietly.

Now the curved doors were open. From where he was, Bond could not see down the shaft, but within seconds the first man was out and putting on his snowshoes, and the second followed. Snowshoes! Bond's heart missed a beat. He had forgotten them! They must be hidden back there in the bushes. Blasted fool! Would they notice?

The two men came slowly toward him, delicately placing their feet. When he was about twenty feet away, the leading man said something softly in what sounded like Russian. When Bond did not reply, the two men stopped in their tracks. They stared at him in astonishment, waiting perhaps for the answer to a password. Bond sensed trouble. He whipped out his gun and moved toward them, crouching. 'Hands up.' He gestured with the muzzle of the Colt. The leading man shouted an order and threw himself forward. At the same time the second man made a dash back toward the hide-out. A rifle boomed from among the trees and the man's right leg buckled under him. The men from the Station broke cover and came running. Bond fell to one knee and clubbed upward with his gun-barrel at the hurtling body. It made contact, but then the man was on him. Bond saw fingernails flashing toward his eyes, ducked, and ran into an uppercut. Now a hand was at his right wrist and his gun was being slowly turned on him. Not wanting to kill, he had kept the safety catch up. He tried to get his thumb to it. A boot hit him in the side of the head, and he let the gun go and fell back. Through a red mist he saw the muzzle of the gun pointing at his face. The thought flashed through his mind that he was going to die—die for showing mercy! . . .

Suddenly the gun muzzle had gone and the weight of the

man was off him. Bond got to his knees and then to his feet. The body, spread-eagled in the grass beside him, gave a last kick. There were bloody rents in the back of the dungarees. Bond looked around. The four men from the Station were in a group. Bond undid the strap of his crash helmet and rubbed the side of his head. He said, 'Well, thanks. Who did it?'

Nobody answered. The men looked embarrassed.

Bond walked toward them, puzzled. 'What's up?'

Suddenly Bond caught a trace of movement behind the men. An extra leg showed—a woman's leg. Bond laughed out loud. The men grinned sheepishly and looked behind them. Mary Ann Russell, in a brown shirt and black jeans, came out from behind them with her hands up. One of the hands held what looked like a ·22 target pistol. She brought her hands down and tucked the pistol into the top of her jeans. She came up to Bond. She said anxiously, 'You won't blame anybody, will you? I just wouldn't let them leave this morning without me.' Her eyes pleaded. 'Rather lucky I did come, really. I mean, I just happened to get to you first. No one wanted to shoot for fear of hitting you.'

Bond smiled into her eyes. He said, 'If you hadn't come, I'd have had to break that dinner date.' He turned back to the men, his voice business-like. 'All right. One of you take the motor-bike and report the gist of this to Colonel Schreiber. Say we're waiting for his team before we take a look at the hide-out. And would he include a couple of anti-sabotage men. That shaft may be booby-trapped. All right?'

Bond took the girl by the arm. He said, 'Come over here. I want to show you a bird's nest.'

'Is that an order?'

'Yes.'

On Slay Down

MICHAEL GILBERT

◆

Michael Gilbert's considerable reputation as a writer of detective novels should not be allowed to obscure the fact that in recent years he has also written some excellent spy stories. They are particularly interesting in that, while the manner is urbane, even courtly, the matter is as tough as any to be found in the work of the post-Fleming, pseudo-realistic school.

If secondary titles were still fashionable, one might, with Mr Fleming's permission, entitle this example of Mr Gilbert's work, 'On Slay Down, or The Recruitment of 008'.

◆

'The young man of to-day,' said Mr Behrens, 'is physically stronger and fitter than his father. He can run a mile quicker—'

'A useful accomplishment,' agreed Mr Calder.

'He can put a weight farther, can jump higher, and will probably live longer.'

'Not as long as the young lady of to-day,' said Mr Calder. '*They* have a look of awful vitality.'

'Nevertheless,' said Mr Behrens—he and Mr Calder, being very old friends, did not so much answer as override each other; frequently they both spoke at once—'nevertheless he is, in one important way, inferior to the older generation. He is mentally softer—'

'Morally, too.'

'The two things go together. He has the weaknesses which

213

go with his strength. He is tolerant—but he is flabby. He is intelligent—but he is timid. He is made out of cast iron, not steel.'

'Stop generalizing,' said Mr Calder. 'What's worrying you?'

'The future of our service,' said Mr Behrens.

Mr Calder considered the matter, at the same time softly scratching the head of his deerhound, Rasselas, who lay on the carpet beside his chair.

Mr Behrens, who lived down in the valley, had walked up, as he did regularly on Tuesday afternoons, to take tea with Mr Calder in his cottage on the hilltop.

'You're not often right,' said Mr Calder, at last.

'Thank you.'

'You could be on this occasion. I saw Fortescue yesterday.'

'Yes,' said Mr Behrens. 'He told me you had been to see him. I meant to ask you about that. What did he want?'

'There's a woman. She has to be killed.'

Rasselas flicked his right ear at an intrusive fly; then, when this proved ineffective, growled softly and shook his head.

'Anyone I know?' said Mr Behrens.

'I'm not sure. Her name, at the moment, is Lipper—Maria Lipper. She lives in Woking and is known there as Mrs Lipper, although I don't *think* she has ever been married. She has worked as a typist and filing clerk at the Air Ministry since— oh, since well before the last war.'

Both Mr Behrens and Mr Calder spoke of the 'last war' in terms of very slight derogation. It had not been *their* war.

'And how long has she been working for them?'

'Certainly for ten years, possibly more. Security got on to her in the end by selective coding, and that, as you know, is a very slow process.'

'And not one which a jury would understand or accept.'

'Oh, certainly not,' said Mr Calder. 'Certainly not. There

could be no question here of judicial process. Maria is a season ticket holder, not a commuter.'

By this Mr Calder meant that Maria Lipper was an agent who collected, piecemeal, all information which came her way, and passed it on at long intervals of months or even years. No messengers came to her. When she had sufficient to interest her masters, she would take it to a collecting point and leave it. Occasional sums of money would come to her through the post.

'It is a thousand pities,' added Mr Calder, 'that they did not get on to her a little sooner—before Operation Prometheus Unbound came off the drawing board.'

'Do you think she knows about *that?*'

'I'm afraid so,' said Mr Calder. 'I wasn't directly concerned. Buchanan was in charge. But it was her section that did the Prometheus typing, and when he found out that she had asked for an urgent contact, I think—I really think—he was justified in getting worried.'

'What is he going to do about it?'

'The contact has been short-circuited. I am taking his place. Two days from now Mrs Lipper is driving down to Portsmouth for a short holiday. She plans to leave Woking very early— she likes clear roads to drive on—and she will be crossing Salisbury Plain at six o'clock. Outside Upavon she turns off the main road. The meeting place is a barn at the top of the track. She has stipulated for a payment of five hundred pounds in one-pound notes. Incidentally, she has never, before, been paid more than fifty.'

'You must be right,' said Mr Behrens. 'I imagine that I am to cover you here. Fortunately my aunt is taking the waters at Harrogate.'

'If you would.'

'The same arrangements as usual.'

'The key will be on the ledge over the woodshed door.'

'You'd better warn Rasselas to expect me. Last time he got it into his head that I was a burglar.'

The great hound looked up at the mention of his name and grinned, showing his long white incisors.

'You needn't worry about Rasselas,' said Mr Calder. 'I'll take him with me. He enjoys an expedition. All the same, it *is* a sad commentary on the younger generation that a man of my age has to be sent out on a trip like this.'

'Exactly what I was saying. Where did you put the back-gammon board?'

Mr Calder left his cottage at dusk on the following evening. He drove off in the direction of Gravesend, crossed the river by the ferry, and made a circle round London, recrossing the Thames at Reading. He drove his inconspicuous car easily and efficiently. Rasselas lay across the back seat, between a sleeping-bag and a portmanteau. He was used to road travel, and slept most of the way.

At midnight the car rolled down the broad High Street of Marlborough and out on to the Pewsey Road. A soft, golden moon made a mockery of its headlights.

A mile from Upavon, Mr Calder pulled up at the side of the road, and studied the 1/25,000 range map with which he had been supplied. The track leading to the barn was clearly shown. But he had marked a different, and roundabout way by which the rendezvous could be approached. This involved taking the next road to the right, following it for a quarter of a mile, then finding a field track—it was no more than a dotted line even on his large-scale map—which would take him up a small re-entrant. The track appeared to stop just short of the circular contour which marked the top of the down. Across it, as Mr

Calder had seen when he examined the map, ran, in straggling gothic lettering, the words Slay Down.

The entrance to the track had been shut off by a gate, and was indistinguishable from the entrance to a field. The gate was padlocked, too, but Mr Calder dealt with this by lifting it off its hinges. It was a heavy gate, but he shifted it with little apparent effort. There were surprising reserves of strength in his barrel-shaped body, thick arms, and plump hands.

After a month of fine weather the track, though rutted, was rock hard. Mr Calder ran up it until the banks on either side had levelled out and he guessed that he was approaching the top of the rise. There he backed his car into a thicket. For the last part of the journey he had been travelling without lights.

Now he switched off the engine, opened the car door, and sat listening.

At first the silence seemed complete. Then, as the singing of the engine died in his ears, the sounds of the night reasserted themselves. A nightjar screamed; an owl hooted. The creatures of the dark, momentarily frozen by the arrival among them of this great palpitating steel-and-glass animal, started to move again. A mile away across the valley, where farms stood and people lived, a dog barked.

Mr Calder took his sleeping-bag out of the back of the car and unrolled it. He took off his coat and shoes, loosened his tie, and wriggled down into the bag. Rasselas lay down too, his nose a few inches from Mr Calder's head.

In five minutes the man was asleep. When he woke he knew what had roused him. Rasselas had growled, very softly, a little rumbling, grumbling noise which meant that something had disturbed him. It was not the growl of imminent danger. It was a tentative alert.

Mr Calder raised his head. During the time he had been

asleep the wind had risen a little, and was blowing up dark clouds and sending them scudding across the face of the moon; the shadows on the bare down were horsemen, warriors with horned helmets riding horses with flying manes and tails. Rasselas was following them with his eyes, head cocked. It was as if, behind the piping of the wind, he could hear, pitched too high for human ears, the shrill note of a trumpet.

'They're ghosts,' said Mr Calder calmly. 'They won't hurt us.' He lay down, and was soon asleep again.

It was five o'clock, and light was coming back into the sky when he woke. It took him five minutes to dress himself and roll up his sleeping-bag. His movements seemed unhurried, but he lost no time.

From the back of the car he took a Greener ·25 calibre rifle, and clipped on a telescopic sight, which he took from a leather case. A handful of nickel-capped ammunition went into his jacket pocket. Tucking the rifle under his arm, he walked cautiously towards the brow of the hill. From the brow, a long, thin line of trees, based in scrub, led down to the barn, whose red-brown roof could now just be seen over the convex slope of the hill.

Mr Calder thought that the arrangement was excellent. 'Made to measure,' was the expression he used. The scrub was thickest round the end tree of the windbreak, and here he propped up the rifle, and then walked the remaining distance to the wall of the barn. He noted that the distance was thirty-three yards.

In front of the barn the path, coming up from the main road, opened out into a flat space, originally a cattle yard, but now missing one wall.

She'll drive in here, thought Mr Calder. And she'll turn the car, ready to get away. They always do that. After a bit, she'll get out of the car and she'll stand, watching for me to come up the road.

When he got level with the barn he saw something that was not marked on the map. It was another track, which came across the down, and had been made quite recently by Army vehicles from the Gunnery School. A litter of ammunition boxes, empty cigarette cartons, and a rusty brew can suggested that the Army had taken over the barn as a staging point for their manoeuvres. It was an additional fact. Something to be noted. Mr Calder didn't think that it affected his plans. A civilian car, coming from the road, would be most unlikely to take this track, a rough affair seamed with the marks of Bren carriers and light tanks.

Mr Calder returned to the end of the trees, and spent some minutes piling a few large stones and a log into a small breast-work. He picked up the rifle and set the sights carefully to thirty-five yards. Then he sat down, with his back to the tree, and lit a cigarette. Rasselas lay down beside him.

Mrs Lipper arrived at ten to six.

She drove up the track from the road, and Mr Calder was interested to see that she behaved almost exactly as he had predicted. She drove her car into the yard, switched off the engine, and sat for a few minutes. Then she opened the car door and got out.

Mr Calder snuggled down behind the barrier, moved his rifle forward a little, and centred the sight on Mrs Lipper's left breast.

It was at this moment that he heard the truck coming. It was, he thought, a fifteen-hundredweight truck, and it was coming quite slowly along the rough track towards the barn.

Mr Calder laid down the rifle and rose to his knees. The truck engine had stopped. From his position of vantage he could see, although Mrs Lipper could not, a figure in battledress getting out of the truck. It was, he thought, an officer. He was carrying a light rifle, and it was clear that he was after rabbits. Indeed, as Mr Calder watched, the young man raised his rifle, then lowered it again.

Mr Calder was interested, even in the middle of his extreme irritation, to see that the officer had aimed at a thicket almost directly in line with the barn.

Three minutes passed in silence. Mrs Lipper looked twice at her watch. Mr Calder lay down again in a firing position. He had decided to wait. It was a close decision, but he was used to making close decisions, and he felt certain that this one was right.

The hidden rifle spoke; and Mr Calder squeezed the trigger of his own. So rapid was his reaction that it sounded like a shot and an echo. In front of his eyes, Mrs Lipper folded on to the ground. She did not fall. It was quite a different movement. It was as though a puppet-master, who had previously held the strings taut, had let them drop and a puppet had tumbled to the ground, arms, legs and head disjointed.

A moment later the hidden rifle spoke again. Mr Calder smiled to himself. The timing, he thought, had been perfect. He was quietly packing away the telescopic sight, dismantling the small redoubt he had created, and obliterating all signs of his presence. Five minutes later he was back in his car. He had left it facing outwards and downhill, and all he had to do was take off the handbrake, and start rolling down the track. This was the trickiest moment in the whole operation. It took three minutes to lift the gate, drive the car through, and replace the gate. During the whole of that time no one appeared on the road in either direction.

'And that,' said Mr Calder, some three days later to Mr Fortescue, 'was that.' Mr Fortescue was a square, sagacious-looking man, and was manager of the Westminster branch of the London and Home Counties Bank. No one seeing Mr Fortescue would have mistaken him for anything but a bank manager; although, in fact, he had certain other, quite important functions.

'I was sorry, in a way, to saddle the boy with it, but I hadn't any choice.'

'He took your shot as the echo of his?'

'Apparently. Anyway, he went on shooting.'

'You contemplated that he would find the body—either then, or later.'

'Certainly.'

'And would assume that he had been responsible—accidentally, of course.'

'I think that he should receive a good deal of sympathy. He had a perfect right to shoot rabbits. The rough shooting belongs to the School of Artillery. The woman was trespassing on War Department Property. Indeed, the police will be in some difficulty in concluding why she was there at all.'

'I expect they would have been,' said Mr Fortescue, 'if her body had been discovered.'

Mr Calder looked at him.

'You mean,' he said at last, 'that no one has been near the barn in the last four days?'

'On the contrary. One of the Troops of the Seventeenth Field Regiment, to which your intrusive Subaltern belongs, visited the barn two days later. It was their gun position. The barn itself was the troop command post.'

'Either,' said Mr Calder, 'they were very unobservant

soldiers, or one is driven to the conclusion that the body had been moved.'

'I was able,' said Mr Fortescue, 'through my influence with the Army, to attend the firing as an additional umpire, in uniform. I had plenty of time on my hands, and was able to make a thorough search of the area.'

'I see,' said Mr Calder. 'Yes. It opens up an interesting field of speculation, doesn't it?'

'Very interesting,' said Mr Fortescue. 'In—er—one or two different directions.'

'Have you discovered the name of the officer who was out shooting?'

'He is a National Service boy. A Lieutenant Blaikie. He is in temporary command of C Troop of A Battery—it would normally be a Captain, but they are short of officers. His Colonel thinks very highly of him. He says that he is a boy of great initiative.'

'There I agree with you,' said Mr Calder. 'I wonder if the Army could find *me* a suit of battledress.'

'I see you as a Major,' said Mr Fortescue. 'With a 1918 Victory Medal and a 1939 Defence Medal.'

'The Africa Star,' said Mr Calder, firmly . . .

Approximately a week later Mr Calder, wearing a Service Dress hat half a size too large for him and a battledress blouse which met with some difficulty round the waist, was walking up the path which led to the barn. It was ten o'clock, dusk had just fallen, and around the farm there was a scene of considerable activity as C Troop, A Battery, of the Seventeenth Field Regiment settled down for the night.

Four guns were in position, two in front of and two behind the barn. The gun teams were digging slit trenches. Two storm lanterns hung in the barn. A sentry on the path saluted Mr

Calder, who inquired where he would find the Troop Commander.

'He's got his bivvy up there, sir,' said the sentry.

Peering through the dusk Mr Calder saw a truck parked on a flat space, beyond the barn, and enclosed by scattered bushes. Attached to the back of the truck, and forming an extension of it, was a sheet of canvas, pegged down in the form of a tent. He circled the site cautiously.

It seemed to him to be just the right distance from the barn, and to have the right amount of cover. It was the place he would have chosen himself.

He edged up to the opening of the tent, and peered inside. A young Subaltern was seated on his bedroll, examining a map. His webbing equipment was hanging on a hook on the back of the truck.

Mr Calder stooped and entered. The young man frowned, drawing his thick eyebrows together; then recognized Mr Calder, and smiled.

'You're one of our umpires, aren't you, sir,' he said. 'Come in.'

'Thank you,' said Mr Calder. 'Can I squat on the bedroll?'

'I expect you've been round the gun position, sir. I was a bit uncertain about the A.A. defences myself. I've put the sentry on top of Slay Down. He's a bit out of touch.'

'I must confess,' said Mr Calder, 'that I haven't examined your dispositions. It was something—rather more personal I wanted a little chat about.'

'Yes, sir?'

'When you buried her—' Mr Calder scraped the turf with his heel—'how deep did you put her?'

There was silence in the tiny tent, lit by a single bulb from the dashboard of the truck. The two men might have been on a raft, alone, in the middle of the ocean.

The thing which occurred next did not surprise Mr Calder. Lieutenant Blaikie's right hand made a very slight movement outwards, checked, and fell to his side again.

'Four foot, into the chalk,' he said.

'How long did it take you?'

'Two hours.'

'Quick work,' said Mr Calder. 'It must have been a shock to you, when a night exercise was ordered exactly on this spot, with special emphasis on the digging of slit trenches and gun-pits.'

'It would have worried me more if I hadn't been in command of the exercise,' said Lieutenant Blaikie. 'I reckoned if I pitched my own tent exactly here, no one would dig a trench or a gun-pit inside it. By the way—who are you?'

Mr Calder was particularly pleased to notice that Lieutenant Blaikie's voice was under firm control.

He told him who he was; and made a proposal to him.

'He was due out of the Army in a couple of months' time,' said Mr Calder to Mr Behrens, when the latter came up for a game of backgammon. 'Fortescue saw him, and thought him very promising. I was very pleased with his behaviour in the tent that night. When I sprung it on him, his first reaction was to reach for the revolver in his webbing holster. It was hanging on the back of his truck. He realized that he wouldn't be able to get it out in time, and decided to come clean. I think that showed decision, and balance, don't you?'

'Decision and balance are *most* important,' agreed Mr Behrens. 'Your throw.'